The second book in the *Flip!* trilogy

FLIP!

Beyond

the

HORIZON

WHERE FREEDOM IS A DANGEROUS WORD

TREVOR STUBBS

THE
LISTENING
PEOPLE

The Listening People
15 Cleeve Grove
Keynsham,
Bristol, BS31 2HF

Email: author@trevorstubbs.co.uk
Web: www.trevorstubbs.co.uk

ISBN 978-0-9550100-3-3

British Library Cataloguing in Publication Data.
A catalogue record for this book is available from the British Library.

THE
LISTENING
PEOPLE

Some of Trevor Stubbs' favourite things:

Mountains

Orchids

Camping holidays

Frangipanis

Chocolate!

France

Reading

Jesus

Happy faces

Christmas

The Australian Outback

The people of South Sudan

Other People's Gardens

Walking

Rosecoco Beans & Rice

Writing (of course)

AND people who have caught the writing bug!

*If you would like to share **your** stories, I would be delighted to read your efforts! Contact me via www.trevorstubbs.co.uk/contact.* ☺

FROM THE SAME AUTHOR

In this series:

Flip! On the Edge

Flip! Beyond the Horizon

Flip! The Daisychain

In the White Gates series:

The Kicking Tree

Ultimate Justice

Winds & Wonders

The Spark

In thanksgiving for the fantastic privilege of being with a twelve-year-old from inner London when he saw the sea for the very first time.

The mightiest space in fortune nature brings
To join like likes, and kiss like native things.
Impossible be strange attempts to those
That weigh their pains in sense and do suppose
What hath been cannot be...
But my intents are fix'd and will not leave me.

All's Well that Ends Well - William Shakespeare

Shakespeare's Helena says that even the biggest differences
between people can be overcome. Nature can bring them close
enough to kiss each other as if they are of the same kind. Those
who weigh the possibilities may decide this cannot happen, even
though it has before. But Helena believes it can and she is not
going to give up!

1

Nadia was amazed, relieved and delighted all at the same time.

"Rox! What the hell are you doing here?"

"It should be me asking you that question, Nadia. It's so great to see you... You went over the top, didn't you? In the fifth. You came down the other side?"

"Yeah. Did the same happen to you?"

"Yes. But we can't talk here. It's too dangerous."

"Dangerous?"

"Just follow me; I'll explain."

Nadia noticed that Roxanne was wearing a plain skirt of some dull colour she couldn't make out in the gloom of the alley, and a blouse of some sort – stuff she thought Roxanne wouldn't have been seen dead in, even at a fancy dress party; it was just so naff.

At the end of the alley, Roxanne knocked four times on a brown wooden door. It opened and a young man within looked questioningly at Nadia.

"A friend... from the other side," Roxanne explained. "Spotted her outside. Doubt she would have lasted another five minutes."

"Dressed like that, cause she wouldn't." The young man stared at Nadia again. He was clearly nervous. "You'd better come in... You sure she's legit?" he demanded.

"Course. I know her. She arrived the same way I did... Nadia, tell Seb the name of the Queen."

"The Queen? What queen?"

"*The* Queen. The queen of - well, loads of countries - lives in London."

"Oh. *The* Queen," said Nadia, wondering what all this was about. "Elizabeth, of course."

The young man persisted. "How long has she been Queen?"

"I dunno. Ages. Long before my dad was even born. What's this all about, Rox?"

The boy continued. "What was her father's name?"

"Seb, don't be so suspicious. I can vouch for Nadia," protested Roxanne.

"Answer me!" insisted Seb, getting worked up.

Nadia stared at him. What she saw in his eyes wasn't anger or hatred - just fear. She thought hard: *The Queen's dad. He must have been a king. Yeah.* She had done it in history somewhere. She wished she'd paid more attention to her history teacher.*Wern it the king in the Second World War? Weren't he the Queen's father? George, sommut...*

Seb stared at her.

"Give over looking at me like that! I can't think, like, with you doing that... George... George... the...the... sixth?" she said tentatively. "He were about in the Second World War, weren't he? He was the one who stood on the balcony at Buckingham Palace when we won... only Elizabeth wasn't there because she was in the crowd down below – cheering. Mr Sykes told us in history."

"See, I told you she's legit," smiled Roxanne.

The boy's fear abated and was replaced by curiosity. "What's it like in your world?"

"My world? What you on about?"

"I think it's about time I told you what you did when you came down the other side of the fifth," said Roxanne. "You crossed into an alternative world – a parallel one."

"This ain't London?" Nadia was confused.

"Yes," explained Roxanne. "It's London alright, but not the London you know. You see, in this alternative world, the Americans didn't enter the Second World War – they stayed neutral. The Japanese did not attack Pearl Harbour in December 1941, but came to an agreement that kept the

United States out of the war... Britain caved in in 1944."

"The Germans won?!" uttered Nadia, amazed. The idea that the Germans could have won the war was just astounding.

"King George and all the royal family," Roxanne went on, "were executed – including the then Princess Elizabeth... and all the politicians and vicars – and even the scout leaders – were rounded up and taken to concentration camps on the continent. Few of them returned."

"So the Germans are in charge?"

"The Nazis, yeah," said Roxanne. "But they ain't German here; they're British Nazis – they call themselves the BUF – the British Union of Fascists... There was a revolution in Germany thirty years ago when some non-fascists took over for about a month – until they were put down by their Nazis with troops from all over Europe – including Britain. Now the Germans are the most oppressed nation of all."

"The Germans?" Nadia's brain was doing somersaults. "But they started the war!"

"Hitler and the Nazis started the war – many Germans opposed them; now they *all* do – except for the nutters in charge."

"Wow. So, here – on this side of the fifth – Hitler is still alive?" It wasn't really a question. Nadia breathed out and tried to calm her brain. Whatever. She felt safe with Roxanne.

"Hardly," murmured Seb.

"Hitler died, aged 81, in 1970... of cancer," explained Roxanne. "But his legacy lives on. There are statues of him all over the world – except in America which still, officially, tries to keep out of the politics beyond their borders."

Nadia was finding it hard to take all this in. "The USA that gets into every war going tries to keep out of stuff? Wow! I don't believe it." Either she was really thick, or this was a nightmare, or this was just a sick joke. And the last of these seemed the most likely.

"Officially," put in Seb.

"Yes," said Roxanne. "*Officially*, the American president says all the right things to keep the fascists from having an excuse to have a go at the New World, but *unofficially* they do sponsor rebellion here. The Nazis know it and are threatening to attack them – but they won't because it could spark a rebellion in Europe for sure, and an uprising is a real possibility in any event. We want that to happen."

"We?" wondered Nadia. "We? You and this dude?"

"Me, him and the... er...look I'd better not say too much just yet."

"No," said Seb, looking uncomfortable. "Keep your trap shut."

But Nadia needed more to go on. "A revolution?"

"Yes. Look, Seb," Roxanne addressed him. "If I'm legit, she is." Then she turned back to Nadia, "Worldwide – an uprising of the people. People are tired of the fascist indoctrination. The human spirit demands freedom. The vast majority are only controlled by fear and the younger generations are getting bolder."

"Get her into something decent," interrupted Seb, brusquely. "Before Number One gets to check her out. I'm going to inform him now."

Roxanne took Nadia off to a small room with a bunk bed. It had no windows – or at least none that Nadia could see.

"My room," explained Roxanne. "Here put these clothes on."

"My jeans and T-shirt are not indecent!" protested Nadia. "Everyone wears stuff like this. You did."

"Not here," said Roxanne. "Tight stuff that, like, reveals your curves, is not allowed. They don't go in for the shape of your bum and boobs here."

As Nadia changed, she took stock of her predicament.

"So... so what are we going to do?" asked Nadia. "Can't we get back? I can't wear naff stuff like this for the rest of my life! And the Nazis in charge..."

"I can't say I haven't been trying," sighed Roxanne. "But I

can't flip like I used to. Back there, I couldn't stop doing it – I was a real mess most of the time – but here... well, *everything's* different. So I just have to carry on the best I can, and it ain't so bad really. These people are good people. It makes them happy to learn that on our side of the fifth – what they call my flipside – the Nazis lost the war and Hitler died in 1945. They'll be pleased to see you – and you can confirm all that I've told them... It's really, really great to see you, Nadia. You're like an answer to prayer."

"You were praying I would get over the top in the fifth and come down the other slope?"

"No," said Roxanne her eyes down, "not that you were to come, exactly – I didn't want you to come here – I just prayed that I would not be so... so alone."

Nadia gave Roxanne a long, tight hug. "Yeah. I guess I would be doing the same. Being alone is crap. Loneliness can be, like, really hard... Outside I saw a notice board on the church. It had a thing up saying it belonged to the Hitler Youth."

"Yeah. The kids are forced to belong... The church hasn't been a church since the 1950s. Is it still a church on your side... *our* side?"

"Yes. It has a youth group – a church one. We attended it just a few hours ago."

"That's great. The people here will be delighted to know that. It will encourage them. People here really do believe Jesus was from God. He was killed by the Romans who were like the BUF in his day – but they believe he rose again to set people free. That gives these people hope."

"It sounds, like, you got religion, Rox. I didn't think you were, kinda, like that?"

"I wasn't. But, here, it makes you think. I guess when people are ramming it down your throat... or old folks get all, like, self-righteous and that, you rebel. You think it ain't cool. Well it weren't, was it? But here, when you're told *not* to read the Bible, you begin to wonder why they care, and so you want to check it out..."

"You never did want to do what anyone else said," smiled Nadia, feeling better. "It's great to find you again Roxanne. I did miss you."

Roxanne took Nadia to a place that looked like a kitchen with a wooden table in the centre. One or two other people came by and said hi but they seemed reluctant to speak to Nadia. They were instinctively wary of her. Roxanne said it wouldn't stay like that once they got used to her.

"Rox," said Nadia, with an earnestness. "I really think we must try to get back. In case you hadn't noticed, I'm black and I ain't seen no other black person here. I stand out. It ain't just

8

the clothes."

"True. Black people are rare, but they exist. And, as I said, it's not easy flipping on this side..."

"Why's that do you think?"

"It's maybe because, on this side, the world is far less about just me and more about... other people."

"You're keen on that Seb. Is that it?"

"Nah."

"But he's keen on you, ain't he? That's it, ain't it?"

"You're right. Seb does like me but I'm not interested like that. If I could flip, I wouldn't stay if it was just him. But over there where I grew up it's about, like, having so much freedom that you don't know who you are any more."

"Free to say what you like, I guess," mused Nadia. "But people don't want to listen to you - they expect you to shut up and just get on with your exams and stuff. I've never felt really free."

"Believe me, Nadia. Compared to this place, the world we grew up in is wide open... but I know what you mean. It's a different kind of trapped. Here, though, you've got to fight for everything - you've got a cause to believe in."

"And that's kind of cool?"

"Yeah. I guess."

2

Back in the other London where the allies had won the war and the Nazis were consigned to the history books, the three remaining friends, Tom, Alice and Hen sat together in Alice's room at the Winterford. Tom lounged on the spare bed – the one that Roxanne had once occupied before she left so suddenly. Only Nadia had known Roxanne – she had vanished before the three friends arrived.

The weather was dull and wet and it fitted their mood – it wasn't the same without Nadia. Prof W was in, but he was acting strangely. Without Nadia they didn't know what to say to each other some of the time – with her gone, there was an immense hole. It's not until a person is not there that you realise how important they have become for you.

The bell went for breakfast and then the usual routine of weighing and checking of their monitors fastened to their arms to record any flips.

Downstairs, Alice encountered Professor Williams emerging from his office. He looked as depressed as she was.

"How's Nadia's dad?" she inquired.

"Oh. Nadia's dad...? Er... fine."

"Good. That's good news. So she'll be back soon then?"

"N... no. I doubt we'll see her again."

"Oh!" Alice feigned shock. "She's left all her stuff here."

"We'll see that it is packed up and sent on."

"I'll write a note," said Alice. "We'll miss her."

"You do that, Alice... I must get on now."

Alice went straight to the others and reported what she had been told.

"I don't like this," said Hen, ruefully. "How did the prof seem?"

"He's not himself at all," muttered Alice.

"This is strange. It doesn't add up." Hen looked into his open hands as if the answer was in his palms somewhere. He didn't find it.

Alice bit her lip in agreement. "I'm scared... There's something going on here we don't know. We're missing something."

Tom told them he had been thinking. "If you were going away in a real hurry... like not having time to say goodbye properly, you might leave a note for your friends, wouldn't you? Nadia might have scribbled something for us. Come on, let's look in her room."

They went to investigate but they could find no note, or anything by way of a message. It looked for all the world like Nadia just went without knowing she was going.

"Perhaps she hid it somewhere," suggested Alice. "If something was wrong I might *hide* a note somewhere for us in case the wrong people saw it. She'd know we'd look... Under her pillow...?" Alice lifted the pillow on the bed. There was nothing there. Then she ran her hands down between the mattress and the headboard. "Hang on..." Alice pulled out a simple old fashioned mobile phone.

"That must be the one she was talking about," said Hen. "The one she uses to check up on her father."

"Something's definitely wrong," sighed Alice. "If you were leaving in a hurry, what's the one thing you would make sure you had?"

"Your phone," replied Tom.

Alice checked the names and the log. The only stored number was Nadia's father's and the only calls were to him.

"Let's call the number," proposed Hen. "If her father's had an accident, someone might have his phone and can tell us what's happening."

Alice pressed call. The phone rang. A man answered it.

"Nadia," a man's voice replied. "What are you doing phoning this time of day?"

"Hello," said Alice, "I'm Alice, Nadia's friend. Who's this?"

"Her effing dad, innit. Look, tell Nadia I ain't up. Get her to call at the usual time. She knows me mornings ain't good. In fact, they're effing lousy!"

"Nadia heard you had had an accident."

"Did she? Well, it's all right for her swanning it up in a posh place in London. I told you, I'm in bed..." A pause. "She OK?"

"So you haven't had an accident?" Alice pressed him.

"Course I ain't. Tell her to call later – usual time." He hung up.

"Nadia's father is still in bed and he hasn't had an accident," summed up, Alice. "Where is she? What's the prof doing?" Tears seeped from her eyes as she slumped on the bed.

Tom looked at Hen. Hen looked down, hands in his pockets. Tom sat beside Alice and put his hand on her arm. "What are we going to do, Hen?"

For the first time, Hen seemed unable to come up with anything. "Right now, I don't know... we have to act smart, and we have to act quickly. But smart comes first... Back to my room guys. We can't be caught by old Brean in here and let on we're suspicious." Alice shuddered. Where was Nadia? What had the prof done with her?

"Hen's right, Alice. We have to play it cool," concurred

Tom. Alice nodded and helped herself to one of Nadia's tissues.

"My room," ordered Alice. "I need to wash my face."

"Fine," said Hen.

Within an hour they had come to a decision; they had to confront Prof W. Hen led the deputation. The time for mind games was over. Hen rapped on the prof's office door. There was a clinking of a glass and the sound of a filing cabinet drawer being closed.

"Yes?" croaked the professor in an odd kind of voice. The three teenagers looked at one another.

"Professor," said Hen through the closed door. "Can we speak to you?"

The door opened a tiny way. Prof W looked at the faces of all three of his charges.

"What is all this about?"

"We want to know what's happened to Nadia," said Alice, as calmly as she could.

"Happened...? Nothing's happened."

"Professor, we think you are being economical with the truth," pressed Hen, in his posh sounding voice. "You see, we know Nadia's dad is perfectly well and Nadia is not in Bristol. Her father thinks she is still here."

"How did you–?"

"It's true, isn't it?" insisted Tom. "She's not gone home."

Prof W's expression betrayed his panic.

"What have you done with her?" demanded Alice.

"Nothing," mumbled the professor, and made to shut the door but Tom leaned on it to keep it open. "Mrs Brean," shouted Prof W. "Mrs Brean!"

"Coming," she called from somewhere not too far away.

"Where's Nadia?" Alice was almost yelling now. "What have you done with her?"

Mrs Bean strode across the hallway. "Goodness me! What's all this about?"

"Something's happened to Nadia and he won't tell us what it is," said Alice, hotly.

Hen tried his polite tone. "Please, will you share what you know with us?" he asked.

Prof W stared straight at him, then at Alice – fear in his eyes. "She... she just disappeared," he stammered.

"You mean she flipped?" queried Alice.

"Yes. Right in front of me on the doorstep; she simply vanished. We've been looking all over for her – she's not in the house, the gardens or the street."

"Have you reported it to the police?" asked Tom, but he

knew the answer from the way the professor hunched his shoulders.

"I wouldn't know how to begin..." he protested. "She hasn't exactly got lost – just melted away."

"He's right," said Hen. "Reluctantly, I have to agree that I can't see how reporting it to the police could help – at this stage at any rate. If you were the police, what action could you take?"

"But we *should* tell her father," said Alice, strongly. "And her consultant in Bristol."

"That will be done," said Prof W, "if she doesn't turn up by lunchtime."

There was a pause; no one knew what to say. It was clear the prof meant what he said – he was honestly concerned. Then something struck Hen.

"Roxanne? Did the same thing happen to Roxanne?"

"Roxanne was a very troubled girl," said Mrs Brean, tight-lipped. "What has this to do with—?"

"Yes," came in Hen. "We know she had a problem with self-harming, but how did she leave, professor? Did she flip like Nadia? Has she disappeared and not returned?"

Prof W looked down at the floor.

"She did, didn't she?" sighed Alice, exasperated. "And you just covered it up – told Nadia she had been dismissed...

What made them flip like that? What did you do to them?"

"I did nothing!" protested the professor.

"Were they under any kind of stress?" asked Hen calmly, as if he were a scientist investigating the phenomenon. "Was there any particular situation that might have induced them to flip?"

The prof seemed unable or unwilling to answer, and then something occurred to Tom. Keeping his eyes on the prof's, he demanded, "Was anyone *else* here? Did anyone else do anything?"

"That is enough!" interjected Mrs Brean, irately. "This questioning of the professor will end right here! It is rude and unseemly. Now I suggest you all go to your rooms and compose yourselves and think about how unkind you have been to the man who has been looking after you and seeking a solution to your condition, and all those others who are to benefit... And remember, few other places in the world would do all of this at no cost to your families. Now go. The professor will deal with the situation in a wise and calm manner. Back to your rooms! And I mean to your *own* rooms, separately, where it is beholden upon you to continue with your studies."

3

Bang, bang, bang, bang! Four heavy wraps on the outside door. Nadia heard Seb open it a crack - then wide.

"Alan! Everything OK?" he demanded.

"No. Rob's got himself shot by the Red Brigade. Stupid man argued with them. They shot him in the leg and left him for the Statpo to pick him up."

Nadia watched as several others arrived - including a man who looked as if he was in charge of everyone.

"Statpo get him?" he growled.

"No," said Alan. "As soon as the Reds scarpered I got him clear of the street... Blood everywhere, though. He's in a doorway out of sight - at least he was when I left him. We can't leave him there, he'll bleed to death."

Then Number One noticed Nadia. He stared at her, questioningly.

"From the flipside. Knows Rox. She's legit," explained Seb, hurriedly.

"OK," said the leader. "Three of you go with Alan. Take

some stuff to wrap Rob up with and get him back here. And, for God's sake be careful... and whatever you do, don't leave a blood trail – don't lead anyone here. Got it?"

Seb and Alan nodded and the leader withdrew.

Seb signalled to Roxanne. "You and your friend. Let's see how good she is. Put on these hoodies and keep hidden, right?"

"Right," replied Roxanne. "Nadia, you up for this?"

Nadia's brain had given up working. She nodded and just followed her friend in donning the hoodie.

The four stole out into the night, Roxanne shouldering a first aid bag. "They made me chief medical officer," she whispered.

"You got medical training?" marvelled Nadia. "You're a dark one, Rox."

"Nah. I just know how to tie bandages. Remember – with one hand..."

It was late and a chilly wind cut up the empty high road. The contrast between the never-sleeping London that Nadia had known – she could hear the hum of traffic from inside her room throughout the night – and this dimly-lit, empty London was stark. She shivered. And she knew that that was not just because of the wind.

They found Rob leaning against a bin. He was in a bad

way, and barely conscious. He looked cold. His foot stuck out at an odd angle from the bottom of his trousers; it was clearly broken.

Roxanne bent over him. "OK, Rob. We got you. You're in safe hands." Rob grunted. She examined his leg. "They ain't got his artery," she said. "Otherwise, he'd be a goner by now, but we'd better treat him real gentle. Got to get this bandaged up before we move him."

"Don't step in the blood. Keep your shoes clean!" barked Seb as he got out a pair of scissors and began snipping Rob's trousers. "You," he ordered Nadia, "check to see the coast is clear." Nadia felt like telling him to change his tone, but quickly realised he was short with her because he was scared. She obeyed. She approached the corner, keeping in the shadows, which wasn't difficult in the low light. She could see no one. She returned. "Can't see a soul," she reported.

"Alan," ordered Seb, "keep watch." He eyed Nadia. She clearly wasn't streetwise – better Alan at the entrance. Seb exposed Rob's nasty shattered lower limb. "Give us your other leg, mate," he said. "I'll tie them together to keep your foot in place... And don't you dare scream. You," he ordered Nadia, "hold him down."

"Name's Nadia," said Nadia, gently. She put out her arm and Rob took it, biting down on her jacket sleeve as Seb straightened his leg. Nadia felt the full force of his grip and had all on not to cry out herself. Roxanne took a roll of thick bandage from the bag and began binding Rob's wound as best she could. It was dangerously near the time of the commencement of the curfew that permitted no movement out of doors but she daren't rush this. To her relief, the bleeding ceased.

Seb murmured. "Rox, get Alan to help me with the lifting. He's heavy stuff." She nodded and went to relieve Alan at the entrance. In a situation like this, you just let Seb be the boss; that was his way. Seb cut a strip from Rob's trousers and began tying his legs as Alan held them together. Nadia's arm was still pinned in Rob's vice-like grip. This was taking longer than any of them wanted.

Suddenly, a bright light stabbed the darkness, catching Roxanne fully in its glare. It was followed by the rumble of a motorbike engine that had somehow not registered on the ears of anyone.

"Hell!" hissed Seb. "Where did he come from? Get your heads down!" But Nadia had instinctively thrown herself over Rob's prone body as Alan ducked behind the bin. Seb crouched into a ball, making himself look as small as he could. But it was too late for Roxanne who fled up the street to draw the attention away from her friends. The motorbike pursued her and its rider grabbed her jacket pulling her off her feet.

"What's the hurry?" Nadia heard the rider shout.

"A blooming winkie," whispered Seb. "Time to pray!"

Nadia was in no doubt that that was exactly what he was doing. Rox was in need of as much help as she could get. "What's a winkie?" breathed Nadia. "What will he do to her?"

"A curfew officer. And he'll do nothing to Rox because he won't get a chance," Alan whispered. "Stay with Rob." He looked at Seb who nodded. The rider had dismounted, pulled Roxanne back to her feet and pushed her against a brick wall. He sneered. "What's a young girl like you doing out on the streets after curfew? You looking for customers?"

"No," replied Roxanne defiantly. "I've got to go to look after me nan. She's sick. Get your hands off me! Let me go!"

"Not before I've searched you, Red Riding hood." He began to pass his hands over her body. Roxanne spat a word that she hadn't learnt from her teachers at school. "Feisty, eh? That'll—" but he never finished his sentence. Alan's left hand covered his mouth and his right hand encircled his waist and pulled backwards.

"Run!" Alan shouted. Roxanne stood frozen to the spot, yet only for a moment. She lunged into the motorbike rider with both fists but he already had his foot around Alan's leg and, before either of them knew it, Alan was on the ground. The winkie stood over him and produced a knife from somewhere – curfew officers were not supposed to be armed but that didn't stop them secreting blades. Rox grabbed the man's arm to stop him plunging his weapon into Alan as he struggled to get to his feet. The winkie turned to free his arm from Roxanne's grip, allowing Alan to recover and get behind him. Mounting his back, he forced him off-balance and, as the curfew officer fell forward, Rox let go of his arm. The knife disappeared from view. The man landed face-down on the ground and Alan jumped on him and sat astride his back. He called for something to tie him up with. Seb arrived with a triangular bandage but when they pulled the winkie's right hand from under him it was covered in blood. He went limp and issued a wheezing sound as air escaped from his lungs.

"Get off him. Pull him over!" barked Seb. They did. The winkie flopped over revealing the knife buried deep in his chest. Seb felt for a pulse in his neck and shook his head.

Alan stood dumbstruck. "Idiot!" he uttered.

"He got what he deserved!" spat Seb. "He would have killed you and perhaps Rox, too."

"Had to stop him. But not kill him!" cried Alan, hotly. "Idiot..."

"If he wasn't carrying a knife, then he wouldn't be dead," breathed Seb, softly. "His fault."

"No," protested Alan. "I felt it. When I sat on him... I forced him down." He sobbed.

"Not your fault," came in Roxanne, covered in tears, too. "You were trying to control him – you had no idea."

"Should have thought," said Alan.

"Get a grip Alan," ordered Seb. "We can't be caught out here with a corpse."

"Alan," called Roxanne, insistently but calmly. "It's OK. You rescued me, right. Let's get the dude back to the bin. With a bit of luck, they might think all the blood there belongs to him." Roxanne began trying to drag the dead man's body. "Alan, you helping me, or what?" Then Seb helped Roxanne and between them, they got the winkie to the bin beside Rob. Alan still hadn't appeared and Nadia went to look for him – he was still standing in the same place where the man had died.

Nadia took his arm. "You OK, Alan? Come on. You gotta move." Alan allowed her to lead him back to the others.

At last, Alan spoke. "You OK, Rox? I guess... I didn't mean to kill him."

"Cleanest way," hissed Seb. "You had no choice."

Roxanne intervened. "Come on, guys. No time to debate stuff here or it will all be for nothing... Rob, time to get you to safety."

"Sorry," moaned Rob, who was now seeing things more clearly. "All my fault."

"No. Not entirely," murmured Alan.

Seb commanded them to check that their shoes were free of anything that would reveal their direction. In the confusion, Nadia had stepped in some of the blood and Seb ordered her to dump her trainer in the bin. "Cover it over with the other rubbish," he ordered. The bin was pretty full and it wasn't difficult. Incongruously under the circumstances, Nadia had a little pang as she recalled how great she had felt the day she got those trainers new. What a world away that was!

When Seb was satisfied, they lifted Rob clear of the ground. Nadia wondered whether she was strong enough but Roxanne made no sign of having a problem, and since she was the taller, Nadia resolved to ignore her own complaining muscles – she didn't want to appear a wimp. She carried her share of Rob until they were safely inside and when they had lowered him onto a bed, she felt she would float into the air.

"Thanks, guys," groaned Rob. "You saved my life."

"Yeah. Guess so," mumbled Nadia. She'd never been part of anything like that before.

4

Roxanne spoke quietly. "Come on Nadia, let's get washed."

"This sort of thing happen often?" asked Nadia, as they went.

"Yeah. Pretty much. There's always someone to look after."

"I mean killing people. Like, you kill people all the time?" asked Nadia.

"No. That never happened before," replied Roxanne. "We – the Movement for Peaceful Change – don't believe in killing. That's one of the things that makes us different from the Red Brigade... or supposed to."

"The people who shot Rob?"

"Yeah. Them. They hate the Nazis, too, but they don't want a peaceful revolution like... I hate killing!..." Roxanne stopped, then put her hand over her mouth. "Sorry," she spluttered and charged towards the bathroom. Nadia hesitated to follow; she decided to leave it for a few minutes – let her friend alone during the embarrassing moments.

Seb came over to Nadia and put his hand on her arm.

"You did OK out there, kid," he said.

"Pretty rough world you got here, innit?"

"Yes. But, if it helps, I don't believe in killing either. Back there," he gestured towards the street, "it was an accident... but, being dead, at least he won't say nothing. If that guy had called in his mates, we'd all have got caught and what Statpo would have done to us would be far worse than that guy got."

"Statpo?" queried Nadia.

"State police. They could even have handed us over to the Sestapo which is something not worth contemplating."

"What was the dude doing out anyway – I thought there's a curfew?" Nadia asked.

"There is," answered Seb. "And he is... was... a winkie."

"A what?"

"A winkie – curfew officer. It's the job of winkies to catch folk out at night. But they're not supposed to be armed because the Statpo don't want no rivals."

Roxanne returned, faced washed. Seb looked her in the eye. "Better?" he asked. "You did good running up the road taking him away from us. That was brave."

"Thanks." A compliment from Seb had to count. After the action, he could be a thoughtful guy.

"Your friend's cool, too," Seb added.

"Thanks," returned Nadia, curtly. This boy was OK but he was kinda damaged, she thought. Doing this sort of stuff, when it really wasn't what a person would choose to do if it were a free world, was bound to warp things inside a guy's head.

Seb took himself off back to his guard duties. Nadia asked why they called curfew officers winkies. Rox explained that it came from the Scottish rhyme *Wee Willie Winkie*. Nadia began to smile. "Who?" she chortled.

"Ain't you heard the rhyme? It's about a bloke running through the town checking all the kids are asleep."

"No, I ain't heard that one," Nadia's mood had cheered up. "Where'd he get a name like that? It's, like, he's got a titchy—"

"Nadia! Your mind!... Nadia, I'm so glad you're here." Nadia's 'mind' had taken the awful tension out of the air. She was what Rox's late old granny would have called a tonic.

People were gathering around to get Rob properly strapped up.

"You people. You work good as a team. People look after each other," Nadia remarked.

"Yeah," agreed Roxanne. "People here care about each other. They care about everyone... well, nearly everyone. Rob's lucky. He'll get into big trouble, though. Getting your leg patched up in the MPC is not an easy matter."

"Where will you take him? He needs to go to a hospital," asked Nadia.

"Don't ask questions. Let people talk first," advised Roxanne.

"I guess everyone's, like, right to be suspicious... You want me to talk about the news back there, I mean in *our* London? Want to know what's been happening while you've been here? You had loads of problems back there, didn't you, Rox? It wasn't just the flipping." Nadia took Roxanne's hand and examined her arms. The scars had faded. "You've given up the cutting."

"Yeah. Nadia, since I've been here, I haven't felt like self-harming at all. Back there I felt like doing it most of the time. Not here, though."

"Why *did* you do it, Rox?"

"I don't know the reason – like, the doctors' reason – but I kind of felt trapped and the pain gave me a release – for about five minutes! It didn't really help – I don't recommend it. It just makes things worse but, although I knew that, *it* was, like, in charge of me..."

"Some said it was your cry for help," said Nadia.

"Nah. I didn't want people to know and I didn't feel like I needed help. I would've kept it quiet if I could but I was surrounded by people – social workers and foster families and stuff all the time."

"But *here* you haven't got any of that?"

"Nah. And you know what, I never even think about self-harming..." Roxanne shrugged.

"You cured, then?"

"Guess so. To be honest, I never wanted to do it then, really. And now I'm too busy; I've broken the habit. So that's a good thing... So what's happening back at the clinic?"

Nadia updated her friend on all the goings on at the Winterford since she had left, ending with her running away.

"You ran off? Just like that?" queried Roxanne.

"I had no choice. They... they were trying to attack me."

"Who?"

"This American guy called Padget – Donald Padget," explained Nadia. "He's nasty, mean, creepy and dangerous. He wants Prof W to chop up my brain so that he can get the clues to the fifth."

"Are the clues in your brain? Never thought of it like... something you could see."

"The prof ain't found anything through his scans," said Nadia, "so, I guess, he's decided that's where it is. I don't really get it. Hen doesn't think he's got it right. Barking up the wrong tree, he says. He may be right. But that don't mean nothing to the prof. Now he has decided he needs a brain from a flipper to check out his ideas."

"So desperate measures," concluded Roxanne, "I never did like that dude. I reckon he's one of them weak men that have to prove themselves by bullying."

"Clever though, I guess. He's got to be to become a professor."

"There's cleverness and knowing what's what, and they ain't the same thing." Roxanne touched her head. "So much for a free world!" she added with a sigh. "I reckon I shall stay here for always and be part of the uprising."

"And bring about a free world like what we've got on the other side where kids have identity crises?" smiled Nadia.

"Yeah." Roxanne smiled, too. She was feeling better. Nadia had cheered her up.

"I don't get it," protested Nadia. "Like, do you really want to fight for this parallel world to become free like ours where loads of people feel lost... or ignore God when he tells you to look after your neighbours - a place where kids are driven to harm themselves?"

"Yeah, stupid, isn't it?" answered Roxanne. "But yeah. You see, people don't have a chance here... If I ever get back I would work to change things. I would not go back to self-harming; I would spend my time telling people not to take their freedoms for granted... And being grateful for education that isn't all about turning you into a clone, like the kids get here."

5

Alice, Tom and Hen, spent all their time together. The Winterford was closed, the tests were suspended and no one talked about studying. Two days went by and there was still no sign of Nadia. They were just deciding to take Prof W to task again when Nadia's phone rang. Alice answered it. Nadia's father asked to talk to his daughter. Alice asked if Prof W had been in touch; he told her he hadn't. She asked him to hold the line.

"It's Nadia's dad," explained Alice. "He hasn't been told anything. What do I say?"

"Tell him... tell him that the prof will contact him," suggested Hen.

"How are we going to get the prof to phone him?" Alice wondered, "without letting on that we've got Nadia's phone."

"We'll just... tell the prof to phone him," said Hen, decisively.

"We can't do that," protested Alice; "he'll guess we've spoken to him. He's already suspicious."

"Yeah, you're right," said Hen, thinking fast. "Tell Nadia's dad, she's gone away and you don't know where. Ask him to ring Prof W."

"Yeah," said Alice. "That's the truth. It's better to tell the truth."

"But don't say she's flipped out of existence. That's too much all at once," put in Tom.

"Yeah. Got you..." Alice took the phone off hold. "Mr Simpson? The thing is that Nadia's not here. She's gone. We don't know where she is... No, sorry, no idea. She left the youth club early and we haven't seen her since... No, it's been, like, a couple of days... No, I don't know why you haven't been informed; you need to phone the professor... Oh, I see, and she keeps telling you he's unavailable. Look, why don't you say you're from the bank or something. I think Mrs Brean doesn't want him bothered but if you were from the bank... Yeah, I know, but she can be like that... I agree. But I'm... no, I'm just her friend... sixteen, same year as Nadia... OK. Bye." Alice closed the phone. "Mrs Brean won't let him speak to Prof W. He says, as Nadia's father, he should be put straight through. He was cross with me until he realised I was only her friend."

"You did well Alice," complimented Hen.

Then they heard the house phone ring, followed by distant muffled voices. They hoped Mrs Brean had put Nadia's dad through this time – not that that would help them find Nadia.

Alice sighed. "Oh, Nadia. Where are you?"

6

At her desk in The Episcopal Church's headquarters in New York, Bishop Rowena's screen blinked a message that she had an email on the personal account which very few people outside of her family knew about. It was from Christopher Hengrove-Blunt and simply said, "Hi. I'm dying for cheesy chips. Hen." She replied immediately but she knew he probably wouldn't see her message for many hours. She tried ringing his mobile. If by chance he had it with him, she was ready to talk in some kind of coded language. It was turned off as she expected – it was almost certainly locked in the prof's drawer where it was only released for an hour a day.

It was so frustrating not being able just to phone or text... and Rowena was in New York. But, then, a solution occurred to her. Like the Episcopal Church in the US, the Church of England operated on a system of dioceses and parishes. If she was able to talk to a parish priest in the vicinity of the clinic, he or she might be able to help. She Googled the Diocese of London and identified the vicar of a church that appeared to be reasonably close to the clinic. But it was already late in London and she would have to wait until the following morning to connect with him, so she tapped out an email asking him to contact her urgently.

7

At lunchtime the next day, Professor Williams approached the three friends and told them he was sending them home. They were to pack and leave the following morning. He said that when the news broke that Nadia had disappeared, their parents would all want them home anyway; and he couldn't cope with angry parents.

As she packed, Alice felt confused. She wanted to go home to Leeds. She really missed her parents and the other members of her family. *But there I won't have Tom and Hen.* She contemplated what it would be like after the first few days of being back in her old room and among her old friends. *I'll have Becky but she doesn't understand what it's like to flip. None of them does.* Leeds was so far away from the others. Tom lived right on the south coast in Dorset; she'd really miss him because he understood her better than anyone. And Hen might even be flown back to the Middle East – his school in Wiltshire didn't want him, did they? *And what if Nadia comes back and finds us all gone? That would be, like, awful.* Alice reasoned. *She'd think we had abandoned her and, actually, we would have. No, as much as I would like to go home, I can't go – no-way.* Alice gave up her half-finished packing and went in search of the others. Tom and Hen were already together.

"I was just saying," explained Tom, "Hen can come and stay with me in West Bay. The Middle East is too far away from anyone."

"Leeds is far enough," moaned Alice. "I don't know anyone else in the whole of Yorkshire who flips."

"You could come and stay at West Bay, too," invited Tom, enthusiastically.

"How big is your mum's place?" asked Alice.

"Two bedrooms and a sitting room."

"So it's not going to work, even if my mum and dad would allow it – and they wouldn't... But what about Nadia? That's what's bugging me. She can't still be in the fifth, can she?"

"I suppose we could go in and look for her," mused Hen, not emitting much confidence. "But, so far, we've never ever met anybody else in there. It's not somewhere, you can, like, stay."

"Nothing to eat or drink, for a start," said Tom. "Not, of course, that we've seen it all. But what we have seen all looks the same."

"We haven't tried to look for much, though," commented Alice, trying to inject some hope into the situation. "Like, we know there's a kind of top, don't we? There might be somewhere up there you could live in. Maybe she's stuck... We have to do *something*. We can't just go home and leave her."

"Yeah, I'm all for going in, too," affirmed Tom. "And we need to go together. It's been much better flipping together than alone. If we can find her, great... if not... But if we don't try, we'll always wonder."

"You're right," said Hen. "I agree. Whether we find her or not, it will be a useful exercise in furthering the control we're after and the last chance before we're all sent away."

That evening they all met in Hen's room. They held hands. Hen was the first to show signs of going and then Alice felt her own heart quicken and the excitement rise. Tom held on to her hand hard and suddenly, he too, came free and they were up, floating freely against the grey plane angled at forty-five degrees to the right. Hen tugged at Alice's hand and she followed his gaze. There was no sign of Nadia but she saw the faint line of the blue horizon that Nadia had spoken of and soon they were all stepping hard to gain height up the slope to get to it. The whirlpool seemed a long way below them to their left and, as they neared the top, the going seemed to get slightly easier. It was Tom who reached up to touch the ridge first and, grabbing hold of it with his right hand, pulled as hard as he could. Then Hen, too, caught hold and they tugged Alice up to join them. They scrambled onto a ridge and sat astride of it with a slope of forty-five degrees on either side. Alice looked down the second side. Apart from sloping the opposite way, it was identical to the first. At the bottom of it was a second whirlpool; from her vantage point on the apex, Alice could clearly see two vortices.

Hen transmitted his thoughts into Alice and Tom's minds, "Maybe Nadia has gone down this second side."

Alice smiled at him, "Hen, if I am reading your thoughts, maybe we can call Nadia, too. If she's inside the fifth, she might pick us up." They all tried to send thought messages but didn't receive a reply.

"The second whirlpool," Tom conveyed. "She may have gone through there. If you were running away, you could easily choose to give it a go."

"Almost certainly," communicated Hen. "Dare we?"

"If we stick together," reckoned Tom.

Alice thought of Nadia all alone wherever she was. "OK. I'm up for it. We have to find Nadia."

But then Alice got second thoughts. "But is it safe? I mean if Nadia's stuck somewhere, we could get stuck, too."

"We have a choice," conveyed Tom. "Either we abandon the search for Nadia and go back – back to our homes – and try and live as we did before, separated from each other, or we go through that new whirlpool and see where it takes us. At least we'll be together."

"Put like that, we don't have much of a choice," messaged Alice. "I want to find Nadia and I don't want to feel like a wimp."

Hen smiled. "You're no wimp, Alice... OK, gently does it."

8

Sliding down the alternative side and effecting a controlled exit through the new vortex, the three teenagers found themselves back in Hen's room in the Winterford. Only... it wasn't Hen's room. The fireplace and its surround were similar but the décor and the furnishings were quite different.

"We've come into another room," remarked Tom. "It's a bit like yours Hen, but it isn't. It's weirdly furnished."

Hen went to the window – the view towards the setting sun was similar to his own except for a massive skyscraper that soared up into the sky where there had been nothing before.

"Look at that!" marvelled Hen. "Where did that spring from? It must be very near Lord's Cricket Ground."

"It looks like it's got a giant lightning flash on the side... and a *swastika*!" exclaimed Tom. "Or is that a trick of the light?" The sun was almost behind the tower and it was becoming difficult to make out, but then, as they watched, the lightning flash lit up – together with a swastika – a massive illuminated sign that dominated the whole area.

"Crumbs!" uttered Tom, stunned. "How on earth did anyone allow that?!"

"And how could they have built it so fast?" Alice wondered.

"Guys," said Hen, ominously, "Guys, it's *everything* that's changed." He opened a cupboard door. "This cupboard has all different stuff in it. There's nothing here that's like anything we would wear."

"And it *feels* different, too." Alice puckered her nose. "It smells wrong. It's kind of musty."

Hen sniffed. "Moth balls," he pronounced. "Smells like my great-grandmother."

"Look, there's no radiator," Tom to pointed to the space below the window; all the rooms of the Winterford they knew had radiators. "It's like we've come back to the past... the twentieth century."

"But there never has been a skyscraper there and we won the war – the Nazis never got here, so why the swastika?" protested Alice.

"I don't know," muttered Hen, "But one thing is certain: we don't belong here."

"I vote we should go back into the fifth and climb back over that ridge," asserted Tom.

"No," spoke up Alice, decisively – and bravely. "Nadia's here on this side. I know it. We *have* to find her. And back on the other side, nothing will have changed; we'll just be sent away in different directions. At least, let's go to where her room should be and look. That's where she could be."

"Agreed," said Hen. "That's the least we can do. If she's there we can get her back. Perhaps she may not be able to work up a flip like we can together."

But Nadia wasn't in the room that would have been hers; it wasn't her room and had none of her things. And there was not a single bit of evidence to suggest she had been there.

They were back on the landing when they heard shouting from down below. Two people were arguing – or rather one of them was shouting at the other. It wasn't anyone the three friends knew. A man dressed in a black uniform, with what looked like a red, white and black Nazi armband with a lightning flash, stepped smartly out into the entrance hall, followed by a woman looking like Alice's grandmother in her younger days – a 1950s housewife wearing a linen blouse, a woollen skirt and an apron.

"This is your final warning," barked the man. "These people are your masters – obey them."

"Yes, sir. But they aren't soldiers or policemen – just labourers... sir."

"They are *men*, are they not? That should be enough for you, woman."

"Yes, sir."

The uniformed man opened the main doors and stepped out. He turned and said, abruptly, "Last warning," and gave the Nazi salute. The woman raised her right arm in a reluctant reply and they could hear the man crunching away. Then the woman turned her hand over and made a rude gesture – the sort that would get you sent off a football pitch.

"Men? You aren't men," she muttered to herself, "I would call you rats – only that would be unfair to the rodent population. So much for my grandmother believing women would be better off with Mosley."

Then she caught sight of three young people standing mesmerised and staring down from the landing.

"What the bleeding— Where'd you spring from?"

Hen was the first to speak.

"I'm sorry, we... kind of... just found ourselves here... Sorry, we'll leave straight away."

"Come down here, right now! Have you been spying on me? 'Cause, if you have, you won't leave here with tongues in your heads, that's for sure."

"No," spoke up Alice. "Honest. We have only just arrived. It's a kind of... a thing we have that makes us move from place to place. It's difficult to explain. It's quite rare."

They descended the stairs.

"So where have you come from, then?"

"The twenty-first century," mocked Alice, tentatively. "I guess we've travelled in time." She didn't know what else to say. Why did she have to be rude when she was under pressure from bossy people?

"But this *is* the twenty-first century," answered the woman. "What are you on about?"

"I don't think we've travelled in time," mumbled Tom, missing Alice's sarcasm and taking her remark literally. "The fifth wouldn't allow us to go backwards when we tried, would it?"

"But what we may have done," suggested Hen, "is entered a parallel universe."

"A what?" glowered the woman.

"A world in which the Nazis won the Second World War?" queried Hen.

"Of course they won the war. It was all over in 1944 before I was born. That's a long time ago."

The three stood, staring at each other.

"Yep. A parallel universe," explained Hen. "Scientists have predicted their existence for decades. It would seem, in this case, that the split occurred sometime during the Second World War; before 1944."

The woman stood staring at them, bemused, not knowing what to say.

Alice was thrown, too. *What Hen's saying does make sense.* she thought. *A parallel universe! Wow!* Then she tried to remember what they had done on World War Two in history lessons. She recalled that when the Americans got involved the Germans were really up against it. *How did the Germans beat the Americans? The Americans couldn't have been overcome so quickly, could they? Something must have happened.* She broke the silence. "How did we lose the war? What happened?" she asked the woman, quietly – politely.

The woman shrugged her shoulders. "I'm not saying any more. They're sending in kids now to spy on us, are they? So, now I have sounded my mouth off to three complete strangers... You know what? I don't care! Do what you like with me, you won't be getting anything out of me."

Hen was thinking the same as Alice. It was the Americans that had made the difference. Without really addressing the woman, he recalled, "The turning point was December 1941 when the Americans got involved. After that, the Nazis were on the back foot."

"Rubbish," expressed the woman, in total disregard for her vow to say nothing more. "The Americans! They sent stuff to help us across the Atlantic at the beginning but then, when it was obvious we weren't going to hold out, they stopped. My mum and dad always blamed them – but I reckoned you can't really criticise them for just looking after their own interests.

Why should they send their boys over here to get slaughtered alongside ours? Of course, I wasn't born then... Here I go blabbing away, again. Anyone would think I don't care if I am arrested and shot. To be honest, I'm not. I've had enough of this fascist world and I'm not the only one... So there, I've said it! Now, what are you going to do about it?"

"This will take some explaining," said Hen. "But we are definitely on your side. We are not spies. What the Nazis did was horrible - six million Jews killed and concentration camps where people starved to death... No, we are no Nazi sympathisers."

"I'm glad we won the war - back there where we come from," affirmed Alice. "No way would we ever help them... anywhere."

"The Nazis were horrible," said Tom, vehemently. "My grandfather escaped from them to England from France. They were scared of the Germans coming over to England. After the war, they never went back to France even though the Nazis had been defeated. No way could I ever be one of them. No way!"

"Well, I must say," said the woman, softening. "You don't look like spies. And you don't sound or look like you're from these parts. Dressed like you are, not really decent - if I might be so bold?... You'd better come into the kitchen then. I guess you're hungry. Teenagers generally are."

They followed her into the kitchen which was incredibly primitive and not at all equipped like their Winterford.

Hen tried to explain about the fifth. Alice rehearsed what she had learned in her GCSE history: that – in her world – the Americans had come into the war and that the Nazis had been defeated in 1945. America had developed a nuclear bomb and had used it on Japan.

Mrs Maisie Briggs – for that was the woman's name – listened intently. She was housekeeper to the Truemans who owned the property, she explained. After a while, she said what they were saying sounded a lot like something someone else had heard. There were supposed to be visitors from what they called "the flipside" but she had never caught on to what it was really about. And people didn't talk to people they didn't know much – it wasn't safe. You only shared things with people you knew.

She was curious about the nuclear bomb. She had been taught in school that if the war hadn't ended in 1944, Hitler had had a bomb like that – a secret weapon – that he would have won the war with, anyway. "So," she concluded, "the Americans got in first, did they? They made the bomb before Mr H?"

Hen nodded. "The Russians developed one too," he

added, "and then the British and the French and now a load more countries; the Germans lost the war before they could do it."

"I don't know what to make of you three," smiled Maisie. "This is a rum turn-up. But my Charlie always said that there was more physics you don't understand than the things you do. And that Einstein fellow said some weird things as long as a hundred years ago that were apparently true ... Sit down and I'll get you some milk... you do drink milk where you come from?"

"Yes," Hen spoke up, "we do. And that would be lovely."

The warm milk that she put in front of them was far from lovely in Alice's opinion but she took her lead from Hen and drank it.

"Your world sounds a dangerous place with all them big bombs about," continued Maisie. "But without the fascists – that's something. I'll tell you this for nothing – it won't stay this way. People will take to the streets. It'll be like the French revolution all over again... and not just in Paris but here in London – everywhere. You can't control the masses – even if they have a big bomb."

Tom asked about social media. "Do they check on what you put on your phones?"

"Phones?" said Maisie. "No one has a telephone except

for those in control."

"What about computers?" asked Hen.

"Ordinary people? No ordinary people have computers."

It turned out that mobile phones, as such, didn't exist. Nor did ordinary people have cars for the most part. Mrs Briggs wanted to know all about the wonders of communication on the flipside and lots of other things. They were talking for what seemed like hours.

"You must be hungry," Maisie said again, remembering her initial intentions of feeding these scantily-clad teenagers. "You stay and eat and then you can be on your way."

"But we have nowhere else to go," murmured Alice.

"Well, you certainly can't go out there wearing those trousers, that's for sure; you'll be arrested within minutes. It's against the law to be dressed like a man."

"I'm *not* dressed like a man!" protested Alice. "Where I come from everyone wears jeans or leggings. It's, just... normal."

"Not here. If you're going to go outside we'll have to find you a skirt or something – and that blouse is far too tight," observed Maisie.

"It's a T-shirt," supplied Alice.

"Bearing the letters INY and a big red heart. What's that about?"

"Oh. It's a present from New York," explained Alice. "NY – New York – 'I love New York'... I've never been there."

"I see I will have to give you lessons in survival," shrugged the woman.

"Yeah. Thanks," said Alice, really meaning it. "I wouldn't want to be arrested. That policeman looked really scary."

"I guess he wasn't an ordinary policeman, was he?" asked Hen, "Gestapo?"

"Sestapo; Gestapo is the German name," explained Maisie. "You really are from somewhere else."

"But they are still Nazis?" queried Tom. "The Nazi salute and the swastika haven't changed."

"In Britain, it's the BUF, the British Union of Fascists," explained Maisie. "Nazi is what we called them in wartime Germany. There are few Germans over here. Back in 1944, the BUF adopted the swastika alongside their lightning symbol, and the German Nazis left them to it in 1950 after they had put up statues of Hitler everywhere."

"Sir Oswald Mosley?" murmured Hen. "He took over Britain?"

"The very man. Died the year after Hitler but the BUF has spawned many of his ilk since."

It was now getting quite late. Everyone was tired and Mrs Briggs arranged for them to stay in two rooms at the top of the house – so long as they didn't touch anything that could not be easily put back as it was. She didn't want to be found harbouring them. They would have to leave early before the workmen arrived in the morning.

"I know what those workmen are up to," she said. "They're not just decorating, they're installing spying devices. They don't trust us."

9

At five o'clock the following morning, the teenagers were awakened by Mrs Briggs and another woman who had bags of clothes for them to wear. Alice was sad to have to abandon her top and jeans – the top was a gift from her cousin who lived in New York City – but it was all, including the underwear, to be carefully disposed of in favour of a nondescript blouse and drab skirt and some revolting vest and knickers to go underneath. The boys felt quite awkward, too, in the scratchy kit they were given but they saw the point – standing out was dangerous. Maisie told them she would conduct them to a safe house.

When they got there – a nondescript brown door in a run-down area – Maisie knocked and left them before it opened, melting into a maze of backstreets. Alice felt abandoned.

The safe house turned out to be nothing more than an interrogation room with two severe men guarded by people with masked faces. It was intimidating but, mercifully, it was clear they were not in the hands of the Sestapo.

The three teenagers were separated to be interrogated separately. Alice was taken down some stairs to a room with a heavy oak door. She was asked to justify their presence and intentions. When she had answered as carefully as she could about the fifth and how it worked, they quizzed her about the world in which she claimed to live. She had just finished telling them about Queen Elizabeth II when the door burst open and in ran Nadia.

"Alice!"

"Nadia!"

They ran into each other's arms. Alice began to leak huge tears. "We were so worried about you," she wept. "You just disappeared and Prof W didn't seem to want to do anything about it."

"I know. That man Padget was there and one of his heavies and they were trying to grab me when I flipped. I kept going and slid down the far side and found myself here."

"Couldn't you get back?"

"I haven't tried. Not really. You see I found Roxanne."

"Roxanne? The girl who left just before I arrived?" marvelled Alice.

"Yes. The same thing happened to her... And you know, here, on this side, she's not cut herself once. She actually looks better."

"But this is an awful place!" protested Alice. "The Nazis won the war!"

"I know. But she says that after you've been here a bit you just... well, you just want to help these poor people. Roxanne's been feeling really useful. On our side she felt unloved and rejected – used, even. But not here. These are good people, Alice."

Reunited with the boys, Nadia greeted them and vouched for them, too. They all went around the corner to the safe house off the Finchley Road and were introduced to Roxanne. The five talked and talked until it was time to sleep, which they did on the floor as there were no more beds to be had.

10

Youth worker Mel, dressed in her signature jumper and jeans topped with a broad-brimmed hat, pressed the buzzer on the gate of the Winterford Clinic. Mrs Brean spoke: "Yes?"

"Mel Jones, the youth worker at St Peter's. I wonder if I could see the young people who came to the youth club?"

"Oh. What have they done now?" replied Mrs Brean, in an irritated voice.

"Nothing. Somebody in America's concerned about them."

"America? What...?" said Mrs Brean wondering what all this was about. She lost patience. "No. I'm sorry; they're going home."

"Going home? When will they be back?"

"No idea," said Mrs Brean, curtly. In fact, she had no idea what was really going on with anything anymore – her boss was acting really strangely – but this youth worker was just a nuisance.

"Can I see the man in charge?" asked Mel.

"The professor? He's out."

"Can I see the young people before they go?" persisted Mel.

"No. They are busy packing. The children won't be coming to your club again in any case. And what happens here doesn't concern you or anyone from the other side of the Atlantic." Then Mrs Brean's patience ran out and she almost shouted. "Goodbye!"

The connection cut. Mel didn't like the way she had been dismissed – or the way Mrs Brean called sixteen-year-olds children in that way. She stood at the gate and looked at the imposing building set in its own grounds. Such a place in that part of London would be worth a lot. She turned away and called the vicar. He picked up.

"Hi, Mel."

"Hi. I'm outside the Winterford Clinic. I didn't get past the gate. A woman told me via the intercom that the young people were going home and she had no idea when they would be back – if they came back. She sounded put-out and was short with me and she told me that they wouldn't be coming to the club again, in any case."

"You said they enjoyed the club?" asked the vicar.

"Yeah. Amazing how quickly they integrated. My impression was that they had had a great time, got on with the other members and were looking forward to next week. I don't think it would be their decision not to come again... It sounded from what they said last night that the Winterford is more like a prison than a clinic. Now I'm here outside, I can see what they mean. And, to my eyes, they didn't appear to be sick enough to be kept in anywhere."

"What sort of place is the clinic, then?"

"Big smart place – probably 1930s – three storeys, white pillars each side of the big oak front door, high metal gate with intercom which I didn't get past. Whoever owns it, they've got some dosh."

"Think I should give them a ring? You know, in my 'establishment' voice?" The vicar chuckled.

"Are you saying I don't count?"

"You know the answer to that, Mel. To them, you might even be seen as subversive," he teased.

"OK. Put your posh voice on and see if you can get anywhere. If your USA contact is concerned, I reckon we shouldn't give up. In fact, this smells a bit fishy."

"Right. You stay where you are. I'll ring you back."

The vicar tried ringing the clinic but no one picked up. He called Mel back. "They're not answering." He checked his watch. "The people in New York will still be in bed so I'll email them. Can you see any signs of anything happening?"

"No. There is a notice saying the clinic is shut for the day and that outpatients will be sent new appointments."

"OK. Leave it for now, Mel. I'll try again when I've. heard from the States."

11

Bishop Rowena was about to leave her bedroom for the shower. It was early but she wasn't going to go back to sleep. Her cell-phone jangled a message alert. She checked the texts, but the alert was from her private email account – from London. She read the vicar's report. This wasn't right. The young people had sent a distress signal and now seemed to be leaving but no one had been able to see them. She was sure that if they were planning to go anywhere, Hen would have mentioned it in his email the previous evening. They hadn't said anything about leaving to her... or, apparently, to the youth worker; surely they would have said something if they were planning on going home?

Rowena went over Hen's message again in her mind. Nadia had been collected from the club early and Hen had been worried. And now they were all going home – or were they? And why was the clinic closed for business? Was there really an emergency with Nadia's father? *Am I reading too much into this?* She asked herself. No. *I don't like the sound of any of this; I am right to be suspicious. The professor was not straight with me when I visited... and Hen's dad knows his son and is concerned. No, Rowena, you have to act.*

She rang London and talked to the vicar.

"I'm suspicious," she told him. "I think we need to get to see the youngsters. I don't trust the people at that clinic."

"Neither does our youth worker," said the prebendary. "She's been hanging around to see if she can catch them as they leave but there has been no movement at all. She's wondering if they have already left. She says the place looks very quiet... Too quiet."

"I'm going to ring Christopher's father in the UAE. Can your youth worker try and get into the clinic again?"

"We'll keep trying," Ian, the vicar, assured her.

Rowena dialled the Abu Dhabi number. It was late in the Middle East but Hen's father picked up. No, no one had told him his son was being sent home. He was worried and said he would get to London as soon as he could. *Ro,* Rowena told herself, *you have to go to London, too.*

She texted her secretary. *Definitely off to London. Clear my diary. Book first available from Newark.*

Her phone rang immediately. It was Angela.

"Hey, Angela. It's early. Expected you to be turned off."

"No, I was just leaving the house. Thought you might need me. I'll get onto the airline straight away. Get yourself to the airport. I'll text you the details."

"My diary?"

"Nothing that can't be rearranged. Leave it all to me."

"Angela, you're the best."

Three hours later, Bishop Rowena was over the Atlantic. She had rung Ian Harbuckle again from the airport. He had told her to take the Heathrow Express to Paddington Station where he would meet her and convey her to St Peter's vicarage; he would have a bed for her.

All this would be quite exciting, she thought, *if it wasn't so serious.*

12

Prof W was incandescent. "Gone! Just vanished?!" Mrs Brean had just reported that now all four of his charges had simply disappeared.

"They seem to have left in the midst of their packing," explained Mrs Brean. "I don't understand it!"

"Well, find them!" Prof W bawled. He was very highly stressed and Mrs Brean became nervous that he might burst a blood vessel.

"Calm down, professor, shouting won't bring them back. We're looking all over for a second time. They don't appear to have left the house – at least not by any of the doors, and all the windows are closed."

"They've done the same as the others," murmured the professor, slumping into a chair. "I'm not surprised."

"Others? What others?"

"Nadia... and Roxanne."

"But Roxanne left months ago and Nadia has gone home already."

"No. Mrs Brean. Both Roxanne and Nadia flipped... and

vanished... completely."

"You mean they didn't leave – go home?! You haven't taken Nadia to Bristol?"

"No. She got into a state and flipped – and then completely vanished... Melted... Poof... Right in front of my eyes. Same as Roxanne."

Mrs Brean stared at him, open-mouthed.

"You're the only other person to know the truth," he explained. "Even Padget and his entourage don't know..." He began to weep. "There is absolutely no one else I can share this with... They simply don't understand. Padget – he witnessed it, and he still doesn't get it."

Mrs Brean gasped. "Padget? What's it got to do with him?"

"He was here... when the kids went to the youth club... when Nadia disappeared. It was he who scared her... She flipped... Must have come up somewhere outside the premises. The same will have happened to the others."

"You mean they are out there. Why haven't they come back?"

"They don't trust me, Mrs Brean."

"Nonsense!"

"Is it? Nadia believes I would go as far as killing her to get her brain."

"Preposterous!" blurted Mrs Brean.

"*I* wouldn't - but Padget would. He saw her flip. Went off to look for her... He'll be back."

They were silent as Mrs Brean came to terms with all this. She was thinking through the implications. "But what are we going to do?" she asked, eventually. "We have to report this to the police?"

"And what are *they* going to say? No, they haven't been missing so long. Perhaps they'll come back - all their stuff is here... They know they're going home; there's no point in running away without money when they know I'll buy them rail tickets."

"You're right," said Mrs Brean, regaining some of her composure, and then added. "By the way, the youth worker from the church youth group came to the gate. She said someone in America was concerned about them. I sent her away with a flea in her ear... You should never have let them go to that place."

An hour later, Mel tried again to gain access to the clinic but no one answered the buzzer - it seemed that now the place was abandoned. She must have missed them somehow. Ian Harbuckle told her they would go round the following morning after the American bishop had arrived. If the young people had indeed all gone home, that was the end of the story.

Late that same day, just as it was getting dusk, a sleek black car pulled into the drive of the Winterford. None of the young people had turned up and Mrs Brean had gone home. Professor Williams had decided to stay in case the young people reappeared overnight. He resolved that if they hadn't checked in by the morning, he would have to inform the parents – and the police. He had hoped Padget wouldn't come back before then.

Damn the man, he thought. Then, *Maybe Padget has found Nadia*. But as soon as the entrepreneur burst through the oak door it became obvious that he hadn't.

Padget was livid. But the professor was too important to lose if he were to harvest the 5D knowledge for the Daisychain; he could not allow Williams out of his power. The last thing he wanted was the police to get involved – the professor knew too much; it could put the whole operation in jeopardy. But, whatever happened, he had to protect his own part in this – his reputation within Daisychain was on the line. He thought of McBlair waiting for him in his castle in Inverlochie. She was as ruthless as they came.

Donald Padget did not hang around arguing; he nodded to Wood who unceremoniously manhandled the professor into the rear seat of the car. Finally, before driving away, he posted Wood to wait for the reappearance of the teenagers and to make sure Mrs Brean wouldn't do anything silly.

13

Mrs Brean returned to the clinic promptly at eight o'clock. Her professor was not to be found anywhere. It looked like he had left in a hurry. A half-finished glass of whisky was set on his desk amid several papers on which he had been working. Professor Williams always cleared his desk before going anywhere.

Ten minutes later, Mel, accompanied by the Prebendary Ian Harbuckle and Bishop Rowena, appeared at the gate. Wood had sloped off around the corner but still kept the clinic under surveillance. He watched as Mrs Brean admitted the church people into the house.

The disappearance of the young people and now the professor, too, left Mrs Brean as the only one to act and she quickly agreed to inform both parents and the police. It was, she said, what her boss promised he would do if the teenagers hadn't reappeared by the next day, in any case.

The police took the matter seriously from the start. Mel, as was her duty under the church's safeguarding rules, had already reported her concern the previous day. A youth worker reporting on teenagers in possible danger made alarm bells ring and now two officers from the Met were seated in Prof W's study taking notes from Mrs Brean who was not holding anything back. Hearing Rowena's explanation of what she knew of the fifth dimension phenomenon and the way that her boss's approach had largely been discredited in the USA, Mrs Brean began to see things from a new angle. But she was still keen to preserve her boss's reputation and resolved not to mention one Donald Padget who had humiliated him.

Mrs Brean said that Nadia was quite capable of making stuff up; what she had told them at the youth club about the professor wanting to chop up a brain was preposterous. Mrs Brean was confident that the idea of her boss killing someone for a dissection was complete rubbish.

"I've told you everything I know," she concluded. "I told the professor we had searched everywhere. I left yesterday evening and I haven't heard from him since."

"No phone calls or text messages?" asked the officer.

"None."

"Emails?"

"No," pleaded the housekeeper. "You can check my inbox ... and my phone."

"Thank you. That might be helpful. May I see them?" The female officer took Mrs Brean's phone and began scrolling.

"Is this the professor's mobile number?"

"It is. I tried phoning him, but all I got was his voicemail. I texted him, but, as you can see, have got no reply."

From the middle of the morning onwards, distraught parents and relatives began to arrive at the Winterford. Hen's uncle was the first, and Alice's mother had phoned to say she had arrived at King's Cross.

Tom's mother had been met at Waterloo by friends she knew in London. She and Alice's mum turned up together. They had been hoping against hope to find their son and daughter safely back. It was not to be. Hen's uncle tried to comfort them. It was good to have allies with the other relatives.

Hen's uncle asked how the young people managed to communicate with the outside world; he understood that they had had their phone's taken from them.

"They are allowed to use the computers," asserted Mrs Brean. "We have a special computer room."

"They have very restricted access," explained Bishop Rowena. "They are limited to an hour a day, or something like that, I believe."

"It's really hard communicating," confirmed Alice's mum. "I don't think... I got the impression that they were not allowed to say anything they wanted."

"That's correct," corroborated Rowena. "Everything they say is monitored. Christopher and I devised a code by which he could tell me if things were bad. I got the distress message the day before yesterday, and got straight onto Mel's parish, here."

"Distress code?" asked the male officer writing in his notebook.

"Yes. He told me he was 'dying for cheesy chips'. Those exact words. He hates cheesy chips. It was the emergency 'immediate danger' signal."

"Please conduct me to this computer room, Mrs Brean," requested the male officer.

"Yes. Of course."

She led him to the room where just two desktop computers and their monitors stood on two separate desks.

"Is that all?"

"Yes."

"Seems a bit mean to have just two computers and nothing else for young people these days. They must have felt very cut off."

"Yes. That was the idea. They were here to be tested and treated. With their condition, too much outside input could very well skew the outcomes, Inspector."

"Sergeant," he corrected. "I'm sure it would. You say all

their Internet usage was carefully monitored?"

"Meticulously. The professor has to know what triggers the episodes."

"I'm ordering this room be sealed, Mrs Brean. I am recommending the inspector obtains a forensic team to take charge of these machines. Also, I want no one to enter the bedrooms or the bathrooms the young people used. You got that?"

"As you wish, Inspector... er, Sergeant."

☆ ☆ ☆

During the afternoon, the number of police personnel increased to six. Detective Inspector Renshaw had taken charge. Police no-go tape had been tied across the stairs as a forensic team were scouring the bedrooms and the upstairs facilities. They had photographed the computer room and tested for fingerprints. The last person to use the computers would have left their marks on the keys, so if those particular keyboards or the mice had been used after the young people, the police would know. When they had finished, the machines were bagged and boxed and taken away for detailed scrutiny.

By six o'clock, they had all gone. Mrs Brean had called in the kitchen staff and a meal was being prepared, as were rooms for the parents and Hen's uncle to stay. None of them wanted to be anywhere else until their children were found. Every time the phone rang, they were hopeful of news. Someone had read somewhere that the longer someone was missing, the less was the chance of them being found alive – if at all.

Nadia's dad turned up at eight. He was in a poor emotional and physical state; he had had to borrow the money to buy his rail ticket. Even then, he still hadn't enough until someone suggested it might be cheaper to go to Waterloo instead of Paddington. Amazingly, it was – although he had had to wait two hours and it took much longer. Then, after getting to Waterloo, he had walked across London. He hadn't eaten all day and he looked decidedly ill. The lack of any alcohol on the premises did nothing to help, and it quickly became apparent to the others that Nadia was all he had in the world; there was no one else. Whatever they felt about their own child, this man's circumstances were worse.

Bishop Rowena asked if they would like her to pray. It seemed the natural thing if they had a bishop, and no one objected. Somehow it felt comforting to think that God knew where their children were, even if they didn't.

Mrs Brean didn't go home that night; the night staff had been interviewed and sent home and she was the only one who could act as host. Where was her professor? Why wasn't he contacting her? Had something happened to him, too? If the situation didn't change overnight, she was resolved to tell the police that she believed him to be a victim as well – perhaps he had suffered defending his charges. *Yes, that is it,* she thought. *He is almost certainly the one that is risking all for those children.* Once again, her heart hardened towards them – it was they who were responsible for leading her hero into danger. *How dare they?*

14

After an uncomfortable night on the hard floor, the five friends learned that they were to be transported to a safe house in Streatham in south London.

Seb explained there was no room for them to stay on in the Finchley Road. "The MPC has decided that now you're here in our London - we're going to have to look after you. And you'll have to earn your keep."

"Look," said Nadia, boldly, "if there ain't enough room, we'll just have to make ourselves scarce until we can get back. It ain't fair—"

"I... I couldn't flip - not at the moment," interrupted Alice. "It's like it was when I first got to the Winterford; I just can't make it come."

"What're you going to do out there?" Seb gestured towards the road. "You wouldn't last five minutes before you got picked up. No, we can't let you go - besides you know too much. You know about this place for a start."

"We'll never tell anybody," protested Tom.

"You think you won't but if you were taken you'd tell

everything in the end. You might also tell them a load of rubbish, but you don't stop talking when they do their thing."

"Their thing? Torture?" asked Alice, alarmed.

"In more ways that you could possibly imagine," answered Seb.

Alice shivered. "This world is, like, insane."

"It certainly puts our side into context that's for sure," agreed Hen. "I understand about the flipping, Alice. Whatever we do, I reckon we should stick together. Now that we've found Nadia, and Roxanne, too, I vow we see this through as one... whatever it takes."

"Yeah," affirmed Nadia, emphatically. "We stick together. I ain't leaving Alice, no way... or anyone. And Rox's in, right?"

"She's in," reassured Alice. Tom gave his assent, too.

Hen turned to Seb. "So, we are in your hands. So long as we are allowed to stay together, we shall do all that you say."

"No choice, I guess," said Tom.

"None," confirmed Seb. "But it's for your own good."

Tom nodded. "Right," he said, "When do we get started? As long as we're here, we'll do what we can to help."

"How are we to get to this place called Streatham?" asked Nadia. She took her new found friend by the hand and smiled. "This does mean Rox, too, don't it?"

"What Roxanne does is up to her," murmured Seb, but with an air of reluctance. "She can stay here safe like before - or she can take her chance with you."

They all looked at Roxanne. "I don't know quite why I'm saying this, Seb" she began, "and I have known you a lot longer than any of these people - except Nadia - and I only met Nadia for a couple of weeks..." She was clearly struggling for her words - almost pleading. "But, like, they are from my own side of the fifth... not that I was ever happy there - but somehow it's like...," she faltered, "*they* know what *I* knew when I was there. I dunno. I don't want to leave you lot, Seb. But I feel like I belong to these people - it was so great meeting Nadia..." Roxanne studied Seb, carefully. "That's not what you want to hear, is it?"

"No. You know how I feel about you," he whispered. His eyes began to glisten.

"That's nice, Seb. But that ain't going to happen - you and me. I don't feel for you the way you feel for me - I couldn't feel that for anybody; not at the moment... Sorry, Seb."

"Have you two been, like, an item?" asked Nadia.

"No," answered Roxanne. "But Seb would like us to be... I'm coming with you, Nadia. Seb, there'll be someone else. You'll see. It's best this way."

Seb sighed. He'd already concluded he didn't stand a

chance, but somehow, his heart wouldn't give it up.

Alan approached. "Good morning. Number One wants to see you – all of you."

They followed Alan into a back room. Number One made them sit down – some on a sofa and some on the floor. He, himself, sat on a low stool.

"OK. I want you new arrivals to tell me, in your own words, what we, here, are about. You first," he spoke to Nadia.

Nadia struggled. "D... defeating the Nazis."

"How?"

"Leading the people to revolt?"

"Yesterday, you saw a man killed. You reckon that's the best way to bring about change?"

"We–" began Seb but Number One interrupted him.

"Let the girl speak."

"No," said Nadia. "But he had to rescue Roxanne. He had no choice."

"You'll never change the world through violence," broke in Hen. "Violence breeds violence. You might defeat the BUF but after that, you'll end up fighting among yourselves."

"It was the Reds that shot Rob yesterday," explained Roxanne. "They've already started it – fighting each other, fighting others in the resistance."

"I hate guns," stated Alice. "I'll help you get rid of the Nazis but I won't do it with a gun."

"So it seems we're agreed," spoke Number One. "Peaceful change is our way. What about you, young man?" he looked at Tom.

"My mum has told me that I'd never make a soldier and I don't want to be," answered Tom. "But Alan did the right thing yesterday taking on that man to defend Rox and I would do it, too, if anyone tried to harm any of my friends."

"So not a pacifist, then?"

"Not if it's them or me, or someone else," said Tom, firmly.

Number One came to a decision. "Right. I think we can work together. We are in full agreement with you young man," he looked at Hen. "We want as peaceful an uprising as possible. You want to help us? We can use your skills... and your youth. People tend to overlook teenagers so they can often penetrate deeper than someone a few years older might."

"That depends. What do you want us to do?" asked Hen.

"I am offering you the chance to help those who have infiltrated the television centre. We have our people in there ready. They are poised to deliver as soon as the order is given but we need more operatives on the inside. You boys will work as maintenance apprentices. They won't expect you to know anything – you're coming straight out of school. Girls, you will be in the kitchen. We have people in both those places who will take you in and train you – not just to mend things and cook but to take up a role in the operation when it happens. You will be told only what you need to know. You will be based in Streatham and then this safe house will be moved so that if you are caught you will not be able to tell them about anybody or anywhere. Got it?"

"How long for?" asked Alice.

"That would be telling, wouldn't it?" answered Number One.

"I know what you're thinking, Alice," murmured Tom, "but until you feel you can flip, we have no choice. And like Roxanne, I'm prepared to help while I'm here. If we do nothing we'll be a liability. This way we can at least earn our keep."

Nadia needed few words. "Count me in," she said, simply.

"It appears to be the logical course of action," concurred Hen. "Besides, it sounds as if I might learn a few handy skills."

Number One turned to Roxanne. "Roxanne, what about you?"

"I'm sticking with Nadia and Alice," she replied, decisively.

"Good. We'll miss you here but I think you can be more useful in this new role." The leader smiled. He was aware of Seb's infatuation – it wasn't conducive to smooth running and

Roxanne being elsewhere might be a good thing.

They returned to the kitchen. Seb was not happy. Roxanne knew it wasn't just that he did not want her to leave but that he hadn't got over the knife in the winkie.

"We depart at seven," barked Seb. "Get something to eat." He spoke curtly, shrugging off his previous softness towards Roxanne and left.

"Seb's not come to terms with the killing," sighed Roxanne. "I know him."

"Seb?!" exclaimed Alice. "What about Alan?"

"Alan's tougher than he seems. He'll get over it. He was brought up by Nazi sympathises – his real name is Adolf."

"Adolf?" Alice was shocked. "As in Adolf—"

"Hitler. Yes. When Alan was sixteen he beat up his dad when he tried to hit him with a belt and ran away. He's angry and is frightened of the violence he knows he can command. His struggle is his tendency to lash out and he knew, out there, that he wasn't really in control. And that's what's scared him. But Seb's got a soft heart. Don't be fooled by his bluster."

15

Once they had breakfasted on some old bread and an apple, one of the group issued them with high-viz jackets to help them blend in.

"You're going by bus," explained a woman in her twenties. "The best way you can travel as a group is to be a gang of workers on their way to a building site – got it? Seb will conduct you. You talk to no one unless they talk to you. If challenged, you haven't got your ID cards with you because they've been taken by the site manager for verification, right? Once we have got you into the television centre you'll be issued with all the ID you need. Until then, best pray that no one asks for them. OK? Oh, and it's your first day, so that's why your hands are so fine. Right?... And Alice, that hair has to go."

"My hair? Go? Why?"

"People working on building sites don't have long hair. And, in any case, it'll attract too much attention."

Alice had never had short hair. Her mum just tidied up the bottom once a year. It was almost to her waist and was her secret pride and joy. She put up her hand protectively and looked pleadingly at the others.

Tom looked at the floor with his hands in his voluminous pockets. Nadia knew this mattered; she couldn't return Alice's gaze. Hen tried as sensitively as he could to be helpful. "It makes complete sense, Alice; we can't stand out. If we're taken, far worse will happen than having a hair cut. You can grow it again when we get back."

Alice felt really bad. She knew they were right. There were so many things she'd had to let go in the past few months but she never thought one of them was going to be her hair. Tom put a strong arm around her shoulders. It helped. Alice nodded, resigned.

The kindly young woman got a pair of scissors, sat Alice down, and then just hacked her golden locks off as short as she could. Alice watched them accumulate around her feet surrounding her in a carpet of pure gold that shone against the dull floor. She wondered what they were going to do with them.

16

Interestingly, the London buses were not a lot different from what they were on the flipside – still the exact tone of red. Some things had not diverged much while others were really different; it was an odd sensation. They climbed onto the top deck of a bus marked Battle Square. Taking in the surroundings, they had a good view of the huge skyscraper with the swastika on two sides and the BUF lightening flash on the others. "It's built right in the Lord's Cricket Ground!" muttered Hen. "That's sacrilege! Where do they play the cricket?"

"Shh," whispered Seb. "They don't. Cricket was banned in 1945."

"Why?"

He shrugged and breathed another insistent "Shh."

The bus headed south through streets that they did not recognise. They passed a shop selling kids' clothes called 'Kinderklader' – there were bits of German everywhere and Alice remembered that here the German Nazis had commanded Britain for several years.

They saw a gang of orange-clad workmen and women

scrubbing at some graffiti but it was still readable. Someone had daubed on a bus stop: "JESUS HATES OPPRESSION". Underneath it, a different person had scrawled: "... but loves the oppressor. Love wins!" followed by a fish sign that Alice knew to be a Christian symbol.

Eventually, they stopped at a church with a spire on a round tower that Alice was familiar with from the television at home – the one outside the BBC – but here there was no sign saying BBC. Instead a large board read: "The Voice of the People". Seb led them off the bus. The church appeared to have become part of the broadcasting hub and bore a board saying: "Studio One". They went around the back of it and Seb showed them a side door. He, himself, wasn't to go in. He just murmured, "Good luck," rather grumpily and walked away.

"He's not a happy bunny," remarked Roxanne.

"I think he blames *us* that you're leaving him," reckoned Alice.

"He shouldn't. I told him a couple of times it's not on... Better get inside."

Inside the outer door, they found another door with a bell. They waited.

Eventually, a woman opened the door and looked them over. "You got references?" she asked. "No, sorry. Nothing in writing. The dog ate it," replied Roxanne.

"A dog? Where?" demanded the woman.

"In the house with the white gates," replied Roxanne.

The passwords exchanged, the five were ushered through and taken to a room that looked like a storeroom. Here, the woman told them that at The Voice she would be their only contact with the outside. She took pictures of them for their identity cards and told them they would be issued with them the next day. It would take time to process. In the meantime, when they travelled on to their house in Streatham that evening they were to do so in their builders' guise.

The woman then issued them uniforms – the girls for the kitchen, the boys for the maintenance department. She made them change there and then and leave their builders' clothes in the storeroom so they could put them back on before they left.

"Keep your heads down. Remember you do not have IDs yet, so stay in the shadows and obey orders without question. Oh, and do not group together for breaks – don't look like a gang of five. Got it?"

"Yes," said Roxanne. They all nodded.

"Girls follow me. Guys, you wait here."

"Good luck," Tom wished them.

"And you," grunted Alice. She didn't want to be parted from Tom; it didn't seem right. But he wasn't her boyfriend, was he? Even if the prof had decided it so. She didn't feel the same about Hen. *Get a grip*, she told herself.

The kitchens were a nightmare. They were told they provided food for most of the workforce of The Voice. Alice had never seen cooking like this on such an industrial scale. As new apprentices, Alice, Nadia and Roxanne were given mundane jobs under the supervision of a dragon. The woman wasn't literally a dragon, of course, but Alice decided that the resemblance was more than superficial; on several occasions, Alice could have sworn that she saw the large volatile woman breathe fire.

Within an hour, the dragon had so unnerved her that Alice dropped a pile of plates and she wished she could crawl under one of the stainless steel cupboards. The gaze of the whole kitchen workforce was directed at her and she felt herself blush so intensely that the sweat ran down her forehead and into her eyes. The dragon bore down on her, yelling at all the others to get on with their work. She took Alice by the arm and pulled her out of the kitchen. Dreading the consequences of angering her immediate boss with a dozen broken plates, Alice forgot all about the huge threat of the BUF regime. What was this woman going to do to her?

The dragon dragged Alice unceremoniously out of the kitchen and into a cleaning cupboard. *What next?* thought Alice. *She's going to murder me.* She stole herself to be struck by the woman's large arm that was extended above her. But instead of coming down on her, it descended onto a brush and dustpan. The dragon became almost kindly and pushed them towards Alice and said, gently, "You'd better clear it up." And then added, with a wink, "Don't worry, I've got something far more interesting for you to do tomorrow. But, until then, I'm scary, right?"

Alice nodded. She just took the brush and dustpan and retreated back into the kitchen followed by the woman who almost singed her back screaming, "And don't ever let me catch you being careless like that again! If you weren't an apprentice with no pay for a month I would insist it was docked from your wages!... What're the rest of you staring at? Back to work. We have four hundred people to feed in the next two hours!"

Roxanne was not doing anything mentally taxing. Her job was stacking the dishwashing machines one after the other and then taking the plates out for Alice to convey to the serving area.

Nadia, however, was being taught how to use the pastry-making machine. It was great fun. She was being instructed on how much flour and salt to put into a hopper, weigh lumps of unhealthy looking fat and drop it into a large vat, and top up the water reservoir. The resultant unappetising paste that emerged from the machine then passed through a roller, like a mangle, which laundry workers used in the olden days. Then it went to a press that formed the circular shapes that fitted into baking tins ready to receive some kind of ill-smelling meat mixture.

17

Meanwhile, Tom and Hen were taken to the top of the building and out onto the roof. Introduced to Charlie, they were given chamois leathers and small crescent-shaped buckets that fitted their hips and instructed to fill them with liquid soap from a container.

"Make sure you take plenty," ordered Charlie; "you don't want to be coming back before your break... Ever cleaned windows before lads?"

Tom said that he had, Hen shook his head.

"You what?" said Charlie. "I guess that means you ain't. Well now's your chance to start. But this ain't washing your nan's shed windows, right?"

Tom looked around and could not see any windows – they were outside on a flat roof. But Charlie marched to the edge where two ropes were neatly coiled next to a big reel containing a long length of water hose attached to a tap.

"Put on these harnesses," he ordered. He showed them how to step into the harnesses and make them tight, then fastened the end of a rope to a buckle at the chest. "Comfortable?" he asked. The two were far too apprehensive to give either their consent or otherwise. It probably wouldn't have made any difference - they would still have had to go over the edge.

"Now, you're quite safe," assured Charlie. "These ropes are secured onto this gantry which will keep you at the right distance from the windows at all times. You can move it left and right with your feet on the wall - try not to put your foot through a window, though! And just yell when you're done on the first level... You should do two levels this morning and two this afternoon. Got it?"

Then Charlie led them to the edge, pressed a lever on the gantry which hoisted them off their feet and swung them over the edge. Tom looked down and wished he hadn't. People were walking about around the entrance to The Voice looking no bigger than ants. The lorries in Great Portland Street were smaller than the tiniest toys Tom had collected as a child and which still lined his room back in West Bay.

The gantry lowered them until the first line of windows appeared. Tom looked across at Hen hovering against the background of the circular spire of All Soul's Church. He smiled weakly and sank his leather into the soap and commenced washing the nearest window; he was thinking of better ways and better devices for reaching the outside of the windows than dangling like a mountaineer on the end of a rope with a hose. *Perhaps if the windows hinged in the middle they could be swung open and cleaned from the inside,* he thought.

Tom was more methodical than Hen until Hen got the idea.

Lunchtime was welcome for the lads and very hard work for the girls. People came into the canteen in waves like the waves of the sea. There wasn't time to even look up as they heaped mashed potatoes and meat pie and something green onto each plate – there was no choice of food. Except, that is, for a group of suited men who came to a separate counter and took their meals to a room off the main one. Alice learned that these people were what they called the executives. They had food that looked semi-decent.

As the last wave of diners came through and petered out, the dragon woman ordered her staff to get their own meals. The chief cooks went to the special counter. Alice, Nadia and Roxanne were directed, as their separate turns came, to the common meal. Alice found herself seated on a table with three other girls. They sounded like characters from *The Only Way is Essex* and they delighted in Alice's "quaint" expressions. They mimicked her Yorkshire vowels with their noses in the air commanding her to say more in her "posh northern brogue".

"I'm not posh," protested Alice.

"But you are! I bet you live in a great big house in a street with trees in it?" said a brash speaking young woman.

"Well, yes. I do... did. But I'm not stuck up like you make out."

"So how you come to be in London, then?" asked one of the others sporting enormous earrings that she had to take off while she was working but made sure she had in place during breaks.

"Because I can't go back to Leeds," answered Alice, truthfully.

"Why not? Your people throw you out?" teased the earringed woman.

"No. My parents... my parents don't live in Leeds... er... anymore."

"They done a bunk?" blurted the brash woman.

"Minnie. Don't be horrid," said a third rather more thoughtful-looking girl who hadn't spoken so far. "They could have died! That was cruel."

"Or could have 'disappeared'," whispered the earrings.

Alice said nothing to all this, but the last comment seemed to satisfy the London women's curiosity. If Alice's parents had "disappeared" then it was probably better not to pursue the matter. Alice began to lose concentration as the women yattered on about everyday inconsequential stuff. Her mind turned to her parents and her home in Leeds in a place that wasn't there in this world. When she was at the clinic, she always knew she could walk out at any time and phone her parents from somewhere; she could even go to King's Cross station and catch a train home. If she was really desperate she could have gone to a police station. Here, in this London, she could do none of those things; and she had never felt less like flipping since before that first time on the running track. She thought of that day – she conjured the smell of the hot tartan, saw the white lines swinging round the bend. She tried to recapture the sense of her mum and dad looking on from the stands behind her – but, here, she did not feel any of the excitement that would take her into the fifth. Tears began, silently, to trickle down her cheeks.

The woman called Minnie stopped talking when she noticed Alice crying and Alice became conscious of them all looking at her.

"S... sorry," stammered Alice. "Just a bit homesick."

"Yeah, well... right" said the earrings. "'Spose you got cause." Underneath the brash exterior, she was not so harsh as she had at first appeared.

"We'll say one for ya," said the thoughtful-looking one.

Alice smiled. There it was again – a reference to prayer?

"Thanks," she said. "I appreciate that."

Then they heard the dragon burst through the doors and they were all on their feet. Their break was over and they didn't want to anger the beast.

☆☆☆

At five o'clock the world of The Voice changed. Workers began to troop out from every corner of the building. A few women arrived in the kitchen – the evening shift – and inspected it. It had to be clean for them. The evening shift was a small contingent – only a few of the people who worked directly in the studios remained to be fed.

Maintenance closed down for the night. Gratefully, Tom and Hen handed back their soap buckets and chamois leathers and a man came to conduct them back to the room in which they had changed.

They met up with the girls who had already donned their high-viz jackets and together they left the building, dressed as they had arrived. They had been instructed to take the bus to Battle Square and change there for one to Streatham High Road. On arrival, they were to study the notices outside the Astoria Theatre until they were approached by a man holding a grey umbrella. He would conduct them to their new safe house.

The bus queues outside The Voice were immense, but the buses frequent. Eventually, they got on a bus for Battle Square and showed the bus passes they had been given. They crushed into the downstairs – Alice almost sitting on a gentleman's lap who smiled forgivingly as she struggled not to smother him.

At last, they reached Battle Square.

"I know where this is!" exclaimed Alice as they piled off the bus. "It's Trafalgar Square. Look there's Nelson on his column... only..." she stopped, her mouth open in surprise.

"It's Adolf Hitler," supplied Hen. They all looked up at the massive column topped with Hitler's statue, suitably daubed with bird poo. A pigeon perched on his right hand which was raised in a Nazi salute. In the next few days, they were to learn that Trafalgar Square had been renamed Battle Square after the place in Sussex where the British had surrendered at the conclusion of the Second World War. Hitler had deemed it pertinent that the surrender be signed on the spot where the last successful invasion of the British Isles in 1066 had taken place. And, in an ironical parody of the fate of King Harold on that occasion, had had Winston Churchill's eyes put out before his execution.

"Don't stare. Come on, look like bored workers on their way to Streatham," whispered Hen as he pushed through to a bus marked Streatham which was approaching the designated stop.

18

After what seemed a long time through the busy rush hour traffic and many exchanges of passengers, the driver eventually called out, "Astoria." The five fought their way through to get off the bus. Hen thanked the driver who looked at him in a scared kind of way. He clearly wasn't used to being thanked. On the pavement, Roxanne urged him never to thank or talk to strangers.

"It's an odd thing to do here. Everyone just keeps their heads down. Got it?"

"Got it," muttered Hen. "I don't like it but I get it."

"The rule is," stressed Roxanne, "just don't draw attention to yourself."

"Miserable world," remarked Alice. "What is this Astoria place, then?"

Tom reckoned it was a theatre. "...or, maybe, a cinema," he added. "Looks rather grand,"

"Modernist architecture," commented Hen, studying the façade and approaching the main doors. "I bet it's really done up inside."

Roxanne became alarmed. "We're not supposed to go in!" she warned. "We're only to check out the notice board."

They spotted a board that announced the coming week's films and checked it out. The programme looked to be all propaganda films; there were no plays or anything advertised.

"Boring or what?" moaned Nadia.

Hen couldn't help himself; he turned back to the building and glanced through the door at the ornate lobby. "Yes, Art Deco as I thought... some kind of Egyptian theme... quite a treasure... I bet it was really grand in its day."

"It's terribly run down now, isn't it?" said Alice, squinting through a crack.

"Just don't do that!" hissed Roxanne, scared. "I *told* you. Don't draw attention to yourselves. And *never* sticky-beak. You lot are a real liability!"

Just then a young man approached them. He had a cigarette in his fingers and a dirty grey umbrella in the other. "Got a light?" he mumbled.

"Sorry," answered Hen. "None of us smoke. We're just seeing if there is a Sunday matinée."

"No luck. Not on a Sunday," the man replied. "Are you seeking the house with the grey umbrella?"

"Affirmative," smiled Hen.

"Follow me... and don't forget to *look like builders!*" the man said under his breath.

He led them across the High Road and into some streets lined with trees. It reminded Alice of the street in which she lived in Leeds and she got a pang of homesickness again. *Stop, don't do that!* she ordered herself. After several corners, they came to a large detached three-storey house with a pretty front garden. It spoke of early twentieth century middle class but had definitely seen better days.

They were taken around the back – the servants' entrance? – into a large kitchen with a cooking range and a high ceiling.

"Have you been followed?" demanded a woman with an apron.

"No. Don't think so," said the grey umbrella man "Wouldn't be surprised if we were, though. This lot stands out like a sore thumb."

The woman went out of the door to check. She returned with a satisfied look.

"No stuff?" she asked, curtly. "Baggage?"

"None," stated Hen.

"You really have come from some other planet," she stared at the five faces. "A better place than this no doubt," she sighed. "At least you look healthy and have got a lot more fire in your bellies than most your age, I guess. What they've got, John," she said to the young man, still holding the umbrella, "is freedom in their souls. That's why they stand out... OK, I'll take you to your rooms."

They followed the lady into a narrow but high, wood-panelled hallway and then up the stairs that seemed to go on forever until they got to the top floor. There were two rooms under the eaves – one at the front of the house and one at the rear – with small windows that overlooked attractive tree-lined streets and well-kept back gardens. In the middle distance, Nadia pointed out what looked like a wood. "Is that a forest?" she asked the woman. "I thought London was all houses but it ain't here."

"Forest? Oh, you mean the Common. Keep away from there young lady if you value your life. There are two places to avoid in this city. One is those parts where the Sestapo swarm and the other is the parts where they never go."

"Where the rule of the jungle persists?" queried Hen.

"Precisely. So long as the ne'er-do-wells stick within the limits of the Common, they leave them alone. Used to be a lovely place before the war. The grass was cut, the litter picked up and the Lido was all the rage – Tooting Bec Common was renowned for it. Now it's a dump... Bathroom's down one flight. There're toothbrushes and towels on your beds. Good job you've got friends, I say. Not everyone gets something for nothing in this world."

John – he had finally deposited his umbrella somewhere – leaned on the door frame and said, "Don't worry Mum, they'll have work to do to earn their keep; they might come from a different planet but they won't get away without doing anything."

"Same planet," corrected Hen, "just different times... and don't concern yourselves; we shall do all we can to make our stay worthwhile to you."

"Glad to hear it," smiled the woman. "Food in half an hour."

"Thanks," said Roxanne with a smile. "We have been really welcomed. We appreciate it."

"Good," answered their host, brightly. "Eat in half an hour."

The food was wholesome, the bathroom commodious, and the beds – close together in the small, low-ceilinged former servants' quarters – were comfortable and welcome. Alice fell into a sound sleep beside Roxanne and Nadia, listening to the rumble of the traffic on the High Road.

19

The next day they found their way back to Battle Square.

"I hate the sight of that man stuck up there," mumbled Alice as they changed buses in view of Hitler's Column.

"Well, don't look at him," commanded Roxanne.

The bus to The Voice was more difficult to find. Eventually, Hen found a stop that advertised buses to Finchley and hoped that they would go up Regent's Street. To their relief, the bus they caught did. There didn't seem to be any information as to which buses went where at the bus stops. Alice found herself mentally listing all the changes she would instigate if she were in charge – the buses would definitely be one of them.

At The Voice, they went to the same door beside Studio One – or All Souls' – and were admitted by the same woman as the previous day. She issued them all with an identity card and a uniform that they were to wear as they left through the main entrance at the end of the day, plus a bus pass issued by The Voice. It made life seem much safer, but it also made their own world seem more remote. Now they were no longer visitors but authorised residents – even if that authorisation was fake. Then they were joined by a man who evidently knew all about them.

"If you are picked up," he said, "this is what you do. You do not – under any circumstances – say anything about your role here other than the tasks assigned to you as normal apprentices. No matter how much pressure you are put under you are to reveal nothing of those who have brought you here or instruct you in this place. You know nothing of the Movement for Peaceful Change. Got it?" the five nodded. "You have a cover story? Tell me."

"The truth," said Hen. "We have arrived through a fifth dimension from a parallel world. We talk about our world. We can speak with complete freedom because they have no access there. Here, we are only interested in eating and getting by because we have no choice."

"Good," replied the man. "And you can all stick to that?"

"Absolutely," said Alice, more confidently that she felt. "Because it's the truth. Well, mostly. We do know whose side we are on, but we will never let on."

"I'll tell 'em what a nasty bit of stuff Padget is," growled Nadia.

"Padget?" queried the man.

"Yeah, the dude on the flipside that wants me brain."

"Right," he said, doubtfully. Whatever all this was about it was going to be a total distraction if the girl was taken. He mentally congratulated Number One in his choice of operatives. Ideal; Well motived but ignorant and naïve. Perfect.

"Proceed," he ordered. "And pray!"

On reaching the kitchen, Alice was approached by the dragon.

"What time do you call this?" she bellowed.

"Why? Am I late?" spluttered Alice, taken aback. But the woman made no reply to her question.

"Follow me," she said. Alice followed. "Today you will work here. Apprentices should experience all aspects of the work." Alice found herself on the side that served the bosses. "Your job today," said the dragon, more quietly, "is to serve our betters with the finest food and ensure that all the sleeping beauties stay sleeping. Any disturbance and you come and look for me. Got it?" Alice looked puzzled. The woman winked at her. "Simple job. Just keep the sleeping beauties sleeping."

"All...all right," answered Alice.

"Oh, and, of course, say nothing to anyone here or anywhere or you'll be the mincemeat in tomorrow's goulash."

"No. Nothing. Just ensure the sleepers are... sleeping," repeated Alice, not quite knowing what that meant but trusting that she would when the time came.

"If they show signs of waking, come and get me," said the dragon.

"Right. Got it," confirmed Alice. It seemed that her services for the MPC would be required sooner than she had anticipated.

"And now get those plates here!" bawled the woman in her dragon tones so everyone could hear. Alice obeyed.

Meanwhile, Nadia was being given some instructions regarding a modification to the pastry mix for the élite menu. A white powder was to be added to the flour.

Roxanne was put in charge of the wine and beers for the senior management and was being instructed in which bottles to produce. Clearly, all this had been planned for some time.

Meanwhile, on the roof, Tom and Hen were called aside for additional training. But this training turned out not to be in cleaning windows but in how to gain entry into the office of the head of the propaganda section. "Why us?" asked Tom. The man looked at him, ruefully. Hen supplied the answer.

"This is highly dangerous work and we are expendable. Correct?... And we know hardly anyone in this world – we know no one's real names and we have no relatives here at all. If we are captured, the safe houses we know about will be instantly abandoned."

"I see you are a bright little fellow," smiled the instructor. "So are you raising an objection to this plan?"

"Not in the slightest," shrugged Hen. "We arrive from nowhere and we have to play our part in exchange for the welcome you have given us. Like our friend said last night, 'you don't get something for nothing'. We anticipated being called into the fray – albeit this is sooner than we expected."

"If we refuse to do this—" began Tom.

"You will be permanently removed from sight until the revolution is over," stated the man.

"Of course," said Hen. "That is reasonable. That is the logical implication. But, Tom, my instinct is to help these people, anyway – help them get a world where they can be free. I want to do my bit for them. Do you agree?"

"Yeah," answered Tom. "I guess... It's scary, though."

Hen turned and gripped his friend's upper arm, "It couldn't be otherwise, Tom..." and then addressed their instructor, "Carry on, sir."

"Good. Well if that's all settled then, this is what you do." He went on to explain about a file that should be on the head of propaganda's desk. "It is a radio play that is due to be broadcast live tomorrow. He has checked it through and will place it in his out tray for his secretary to take to the studio at the end of the day. I want you to empty the contents of the file, replace the sheets with these I am giving you and return it to the out tray." He placed a foolscap paper file containing a typed manuscript in a backpack and added, "Needless to say you don't need to know why." He presented the bag to Hen. "You do it at a quarter past two this afternoon, precisely. In the meantime, you keep this bag on your back at all times. When you have completed the transfer you continue with your window cleaning until the end of the day and you leave this bag with your gear in the kit store. Got it?"

"Yes," said Hen. "That seems simple enough. Where do we find the correct window?"

"Four storeys down, second from the left as you face the building. You can't miss it – he's the one who always has his Roman blinds shut and the light on, irrespective of the time of day. He doesn't trust people not to look in."

"At that height, you'd have a job to," marvelled Tom.

"Unless you're a window cleaner dangling on a rope," smiled Hen, with a wink.

"I guess you can't trust window cleaners these days," chuckled Tom.

"I'd better be able to trust *you*!" said the man, with a scowl. "Don't get caught!"

"How are we to get into his office without him seeing us?" asked Tom.

"He'll head off for lunch sometime between one and two p.m. We've arranged that he and his colleagues will be having an afternoon nap... But you'll find out if the way is clear the moment you open the window fully – he might always have the blinds drawn but hates the window being shut tight. If he's there, he'll bawl you out. In that case back off. Otherwise, get in and get out! No mucking about."

"Right," reckoned Tom, "Sounds easy enough – four down, the second one in."

"We'll work so that we naturally come to that window at that time," said Hen. "That way it will not look suspicious if someone's watching us."

The man nodded. "Good plan. Begin your work." And he saw to the ropes as they both put on their harnesses and Hen donned the backpack.

"OK," suggested Tom, as they descended to the first level. "Two levels this morning and we'll naturally come to the window in question first thing this afternoon."

"Agreed," confirmed Hen.

Downstairs in the kitchens, the dragon made sure Nadia knew exactly where her pastry had got to.

"You don't want any of the ordinary folk getting the special stuff," she explained. "Follow it through. I want the special stuff in the élite dining room," and she gave Nadia a wink as she added under her breath, "and make sure you don't lick your fingers!"

20

At lunchtime, Nadia was put on with Alice to serve the élite.

They weren't surprised to see Roxanne was to be the wine waitress but Alice tried her best not to give any indication they were friends; they had all got the message. She was nervous as the first of their distinguished customers arrived.

The pies were especially popular – nearly everyone took one. These particular ones were a weekly treat and, although these people were the bosses, decent food was always hard to come by in Nazi London – unless you were part of the ruling clique. Even the heads of department in The Voice, it seemed, were mere servants of the Ministry in Westminster.

There were two men and three women who declined the pies – and one of them was the head of propaganda sitting with the other heads of department on the top table. The dragon sent Roxanne an urgent order to ensure he drank the wine.

After a few minutes, Roxanne reported that all five of the pie decliners had taken a glass of the special wine. She kept circulating as the company ate their meals. They could hear the noise of the common people's dining room gradually subside as the lunch hour came to its end. The low conversation in the élite section was becoming less but no one made a move to get up. Roxanne kept circulating. People were beginning to slump in their seats but the head of propaganda noticed that things were not right. He got to his feet to protest.

Alice panicked; should she call for the dragon? But Roxanne approached the man just in time to catch him as he slumped sideways. She couldn't hold him but she prevented him from hitting the table on his way down. Nadia stepped among the sleeping people to help her. The man started to giggle. Then he passed out with a smile on his lips and Alice ran for the dragon to report the incident.

The dragon came through and nodded with a wry smile. "Recreational drug overdose I would say. Silly man to take it while being here on duty," she smirked. She placed a plastic pouch with the remains of some of the white powder in his top pocket. Then she gave the girls more of the packets and told them to circulate among the sleepers and put them into various pockets. Finally, she placed a larger consignment into the bottom of a briefcase belonging to the head of security. "That'll take some explaining when he comes to... Now, girls, washing-up. I want all these plates in the dishwasher forthwith," she said quietly. "And, Roxanne, pour the rest of your wine down the sink, pronto. It'll take me ten minutes to report this and when the investigation starts I need the only trace of the drug to be in these people's pockets. To action!"

The dragon left them and returned to the kitchen and Alice heard her bawling out some of the other workers as per usual.

Ten minutes later, Alice, Nadia and Roxanne had everything under control. The dragon returned and started yelling. "What's all this about? Why wasn't I told earlier? What do you mean you didn't want to disturb me...! Oh, my Lord...! *All* of them...? Why didn't you stop people leaving?" She turned on her heals yelling for the second in command. "Janice we're in trouble! Why the hell didn't you tell me?!"

"I didn't... wh... what the hell–" stammered Janice.

"Get security," bellowed the dragon.

Ten minutes later the élite dining room was crawling with security guards and the sleepers were gradually coming to – many of them giggling as they did so.

21

Hen and Tom returned from their lunch and at two fifteen precisely they were dangling outside the room they had been told about. Sure enough one of the windows was open slightly and the vertical blinds inside moved in the breeze. Tom looked at Hen who nodded. He pulled the window open wider and the blinds blew inwards. No sound came from within. Tom swung away to allow Hen to get his feet onto the inside window sill. Still no sound. Hen pushed the blinds aside. The door was open but there was no one in the room. Hen grabbed the window frame and lowered his head; his rope was preventing him from going any further.

"Tom," he called. "I need you to unbuckle me as I hang onto the window frame."

"Yeah. Give us a sec."

Tom pulled himself into a place where he could reach the front of Hen's waist. As he did so he glanced at the road below. He feared arousing suspicion. But what he saw were tiny cars and ant-like people and it reminded him of just how high up they were. He shuddered.

"Tom!" said Hen urgently. "Now's not the time—"

Tom unclasped the rope with his right hand and held his left firmly against Hen's backpack. But he needn't have worried. Released, Hen quickly pulled himself inside.

The file. Where was the file? Hen looked at the desk. There, in a basket on the left top. Then he heard footsteps approaching. They stopped in what must have been an outer office. Hen needed to hide. He got back onto the window ledge behind the blind further along from the open window. The Roman blinds completely covered him but they must have bulged. Those in front of the open window were swinging a lot in the breeze.

A woman entered the office. She gave a sigh of exasperation and murmured, "Him and his windows and blinds!" She strode across the room drew the blind partially aside and pulled the window almost shut; then she left the room but remained in the outer office. Hen could hear her through the open door. It was now at least two-thirty; he must make his escape. But how?

Then to his relief, he heard the woman close the door. Finally, he made out her footsteps as she walked back through her office and into the corridor. At last, all was quiet.

Hen got down off the window sill, took off his backpack, pulled out the substitute folder and did the switch. Back behind the blinds, he opened the window and stepped up onto the window sill. Tom was ready to reconnect his friend but before Hen could put his head outside he heard the woman return to the outer office. If she came into the room the game would be up. His mind raced to come up with a decent excuse, then he considered jumping. But in the instant he tensed to commit himself to what could have been the final act of his life, there was an almighty screech in the outer office behind him and alarm sirens began sounding throughout the building. The woman ran out; she hadn't seen him. Hen breathed a huge sigh. The alarm could not be about him, surely. Hen could hear his heart beating hard and fast but he was free and, teetering on the windowsill, felt the flip loom up. But no! This was madness – there was no way a trip into the fifth was safe. Panic and fear took over and saved him.

Hen shook himself back into engaging his mind over the situation and grabbed the rope Tom proffered him with one hand whilst clinging to the window frame with the other. Tom found the clasp and clipped it in. Safe from disaster, Hen leapt into the open air. As he swung back towards the building he caught the window frame and pushed the window as close to shut as he could. Then they moved on down the line of windows, ignoring the noise from inside. Soaping a window, Hen relaxed both body and mind – he'd done it. A wave of satisfaction swept through him but he had control. No, he smiled to himself, there was no way he was going anywhere fast. All he wanted to do for the rest of that day was clean boring windows.

A minute later, however, they were being hoisted back up onto the roof. They were met by Charlie and two uniformed security men.

Hen looked back over the edge and shrugged. "Problems?" he asked, nonchalantly.

"Not your business. Get downstairs," barked the security man.

Hen and Tom returned their gear – including the backpack – to the kit room as instructed and followed the guards down into the foyer where they joined a flock of other workmen and women. There was no sign of the girls in the crowd.

The workers milled about in the foyer. No one dared talk about the reason for the alarm. They were not asked to leave the building so it did not sound like a fire. Tom and Hen sat down on a step and waited. Tom glanced at Hen when he thought it safe. Hen looked straight forward and whispered. "Nothing to do with us." A phrase that could be taken two ways. Tom understood.

"The girls?" asked Tom.

"Just pray," was all that Hen said.

They sat and waited in silence.

22

The dining halls and kitchens were in lockdown. Alice watched through the open hatch as the security guards were followed by paramedics in peaked caps. They looked bewildered – there were so many men and a few women in various states of consciousness or otherwise that they didn't know where to start. Nadia had cleaned down and polished the pastry mixing machine, Roxanne had emptied all the remaining special wine down the sink and washed out the bottles. Alice had consigned the food leftovers to the chute that led to the skips in the basement - skips that were already on their way to an incinerator north of the city.

Roxanne was helping Alice out with the plates when the dragon bellowed at everyone to get into the main dining hall and eat their lunch and leave the élite lot to those whose concern it was. "What's happening there is none of our business," she yelled in Nadia's direction as the girl finished topping up the machine with fresh flour. "Leave that and get your lunch." Nadia put down the flour and did as she was bid. The dragon gave her a sly wink as she passed.

The wave of first-aiders and paramedics was followed by a

second wave of police. They commanded all the kitchen staff to remain where they were in the main dining room and prevented any further comings and goings. Although Alice could not see what was happening in the élite section she could hear protesting and complaining interspersed with giggling and the occasional scream. The kitchen workforce said nothing. The maxim "When in doubt shut your mouth" was certainly being applied that day. Alice could positively smell the fear among the workers as they sweated in silence, glued to their seats. She soon discovered why.

The Statpo police were followed by four tall black-uniformed men with officers' caps and steel-capped boots. They bore the same lightning insignia on their upper arms that Alice had first seen on the side of the building in what had been Lord's Cricket Ground. Piercing eyes, unblinking and threatening, were set in their straight expressionless faces. Alice felt an unspoken gasp among those around her. No one even dared to breathe as the four officers entered the main dining hall and surveyed the cowering staff – their half-eaten food left as it was on the tables in front of them.

Alice thought of some of the horror movies she had seen – she shouldn't have as they had been given an eighteen certificate from the British Board of Film Censors but her friend, Beth, always seemed to get hold of them for sleepovers. But this was no movie. The four men strutted with their hands behind their backs like black robots ready to strike some cowering kitchen hand with snake-like speed. They weren't exactly going to turn into aliens but Alice thought they looked as if they lacked proper human functions. She wondered if they could smell her guilt and would pull her out and devour her. But everyone was so frightened that no one stood out. Listening to the clipped heels and looking at her half-eaten stew, for some reason Alice remembered what Beth had said when a threatening character had filled her friend's 55 inch ultra HD TV screen: "Just imagine him doing a poo – they all have to, you know" and they had giggled. It helped now... but Alice didn't giggle.

The Sestapo scrutinised the group for at least three minutes but it felt much, much longer. *What are they looking for?* Alice thought. *Not fear – everyone's scared. Guilt? Defiance?... Defiance? What's Nadia thinking? Hope she's not going to get bolshie. Just keep your head down.* Then one of the men – he seemed even taller than the others – turned to the dragon. He greeted her with a crisp Nazi salute to which she was supposed to respond but hers wasn't quite so crisp.

"You're in charge here?" he barked.

"Yes, sir."

"Why was this allowed to happen?"

"Drugs are not permitted, sir, but... in the élite dining

room... they are our superiors, sir... I have no authority... not like on this side. I can assure you there are *never* any drugs among my staff—"

"How do you know this is about drugs?" demanded the officer.

"Because it's not the first time," said the dragon, more confidently. "But this time the drugs must have been more powerful."

Just then a colleague approached the officer. He held the briefcase with the drugs stash in a gloved hand. "Sir!" he barked.

The officer glanced inside, then at the dragon and said, "You should have reported this earlier!"

"Yes, sir."

He stomped off back to the élite side taking his colleagues with him followed by the security personnel. There was a collective sigh as everyone began breathing again and the dragon regained her fire. "So what are you staring at? I told you this doesn't concern you, or any of us. Get on and finish your food... and let this be a lesson to *you* to *never* take drugs for fun!" No one said anything. "Well?" barked the dragon.

"No, ma'am. Never," said one brave little soul. The others all nodded.

"Eat!" the dragon ordered.

They began eating, although it was hard under the circumstances. They could hear the raised voices of the Sestapo as the élite dining hall was gradually cleared of the casualties of the drugs. Eventually, the sounds receded and after a few minutes' silence, the dragon ordered everyone back to work.

Tom and Hen were also ordered back to the roof but not before they witnessed several dozen well-dressed executives and office workers being led from the building in handcuffs – none of them looking very well – to waiting Black Marias that had drawn up outside the building. No one had any idea what this was all about.

☆☆☆

As five o'clock approached, the dragon took her three new apprentices aside and, out of sight of the rest of the staff, gave them a rollicking that everyone could hear. What no one but the girls could see, however, was the smile on the dragon's face and her thumbs up sign. "You," she bellowed, "have come here to learn. I gave you a chance and you have all – all three of you – let me down. It doesn't take much brain to tell your superior when people start falling asleep on the floor!

But, oh no, you didn't. You let it get out of hand – and you got *me* interrogated by the Sestapo. Do you expect me to forgive and forget that? You should be *extremely* grateful that I did not single you out and report you; let *you* face the music. What I have learned is that you are *useless!*" she gave two more thumbs up signs and a giant wink. "Utterly useless and I want you out of my sight for good. I don't want to see you tomorrow or ever. Find yourselves another apprenticeship, but *not* in my kitchens or dining rooms! Now make yourselves scarce." And then she added under her voice, "Well done – keep safe!"

"Thanks," whispered Nadia.

"What are you waiting for? Get out!" barked the dragon and walked away.

23

Roxanne, Alice and Nadia made their way to the bus stop. Great Portland Street and Upper Rent Street were crawling with uniformed men. At last, the girls spotted the boys in the queue.

"Hi," said Alice. They were all pleased to see each other but were learning to show no emotion on the streets.

"They're everywhere," remarked Roxanne, softly.

"I know," said Hen. "From up on top it looks like someone dug up an ants' nest. Let's just get back to Streatham."

As the bus left the vicinity of All Souls', the uniforms and black and yellow vehicles became fewer. Battle Square was the same crowded interchange as the previous day but they changed buses safely and without incident.

Back inside the house, the five related their stories to each other. They had all been at the heart of what must have taken a lot of planning over a long time.

"To be trusted with all that!" gasped Roxanne, "It is a huge compliment."

"Yeah," said Nadia. "We could have mucked it up real

proper."

"But we didn't," insisted Hen. "They planned all along to use someone like us."

"And trusted God to send us," said Roxanne. "I mean it. They would have prayed someone like us would come along to do it."

"And so, now, they're probably saying God provided," sighed Alice. "I mean He didn't, did He? We just happened to come along at the right time."

"What's not to say that God didn't have a hand in that?" Roxanne wanted to know.

"You mean God used us without our knowing?" questioned Nadia. "I reckon I would know if God was getting me to do something."

"Not necessarily," put in Hen. He had been unusually quiet. "Does God ask people to do things using words?"

"I guess not" conceded Nadia. They all became thoughtful.

"Anyway, God or not, we did what they planned," came in Alice – her face alive with happiness now that the relief was kicking in. "I'm glad we stirred up that ants' nest."

"I used to think Britain was like – mostly – naff," mused Nadia. "I mean *my* Bristol and all that, but it ain't half as naff as this place. And what that Padget wants to do is make it like it is here... And, one thing's for certain – he ain't going to do it with *my* brain."

"He's not going to have a chance if we're stuck here, is he?" sighed Alice, wistfully. She was getting homesick again. "Do you reckon we're ever going to get back? My parents will be really worried."

"After today's excitement, we should feel like flipping at least a bit," suggested Tom.

"But I just *don't*," shrugged Alice. "I'm as flat as... I'm as 'normal' as I have been in ages."

For Nadia, the events immediately before her escape reared before her. She dreaded the prospect of being back there in the Winterford. "It ain't safe in the clinic, though, is it? It's not Prof W that's the real danger, innit? It's Padget and his crew. They were going to do just as bad things to me as this Nazi lot. He kept joking about cutting my head open. Only it weren't a joke, he meant it!"

"You're right," agreed Hen. "Padget belongs to some kind of group that sees the potential of the fifth as a weapon. Or at least, something they need to understand to protect themselves from."

"Daisies," grunted Nadia.

"What?" wondered Tom. "What about daisies?"

"Padget and his cronies; they've all got daisies

somewhere. His sidekick chauffeur or whatever he is, that awful nurse woman that does the tests—"

"Yeah, I know who you mean," said Alice, "it's a pretty flower pendant."

"Yes. And the Spanish night staff woman that you call General Franco has got a daisy broach," added Tom.

"Well spotted," complemented Hen.

"But the prof *ain't* got one," stated Nadia. "Not that I can see."

"I would bet he's not one of them," Hen reflected. "That makes sense... But all that's for when we get back. Right now we have to keep our wits about us. We're in the middle of a major event. Today was great seeing all the Nazis running around in confusion but I don't think what we saw today is the end of what we did. The business in the dining room might have been a distraction – it could be that the file I swapped is what this is really about."

"*Your* contribution, then." Alice smiled with mock sarcasm.

"No," corrected Hen. "It took all of us. That's the point. Without the events of the dining room, I wouldn't have had the opportunity to get in and out of that office as I did. And all those important people in trouble is a real coup, but *what is in that file?* That's what I'm asking myself; it's like a time-bomb ready to go off later."

Alice reminded them that they were not going back to The Voice. "Well, since we have all been sacked, whatever it was we might never know," she said with a tinge of disappointment.

"The Voice is the last place they would want us," put in Tom, "They want us out of the way... Safer all round."

"Quite," smiled Hen.

Alice longed for the days when her life was planned out - school years, exams, sports training. "So what now?" she asked.

"Wait until someone from the MPC tells us what to do next," answered Roxanne.

"Like, just wait?"

"Yeah. Just wait," said Roxanne, confidently. "That's the way it works."

They didn't have to wait long. Their landlady ordered them downstairs and fed them. As they ate a plate of turnips, greens and gravy, she explained that under no circumstances were they to return to where they had been working; it had been decided that they were to become a group of performers.

"Performers?" marvelled Hen.

"Yes," said the woman. "Tomorrow you will audition at the Astoria as a troupe of travelling entertainers."

"Oh dear," sighed Hen. "I don't think I can entertain."

"Me, neither," declared Alice.

"So you have until tomorrow afternoon to learn," replied the woman. "You are among the most resourceful young people we have encountered. I'm sure you can come up with something."

24

That evening, they pooled their acting experience. Alice knew the words of most of the songs from the *Sound of Music* but Hen pointed out that that was hardly appropriate since the plot was about escaping from the Nazis and – anyway – no one would know those songs because they were written after the temporal split.

"I once sang a really old song called *Show me the way to go home* in a school concert," remembered Tom. "But that was with a load of others and I'm certainly not good enough to be on a stage in front of an audience who have paid."

Hen shrugged his shoulders. "I guess we 'resourceful young people' have to try, Tom... You know the words? All of them?"

"Well, yeah, I think I can remember them."

"If they've got a piano, I reckon I can play the tune." Hen hummed it. The girls said they 'kind of' knew it.

"How old is it?" asked Roxanne.

"Old enough," confirmed Hen, thinking. "It's an Old Time Music Hall number... Yeah, we could be a Music Hall act.

That's more like acting than singing – sort of light-hearted. A bit of a laugh. It won't matter if the singing isn't so good."

They worked on *Show me the way to go home*. Everyone learned the chorus and Tom put in the verses.

Hen tried to write down the music but he couldn't get it without a piano. "I think you might have to sing it *a cappella*, Tom – unless I can get the sheet music. And this all depends on whether or not they've got a piano anyway... What else do we know that's Old Time Music Hall?"

"Is *My old man said follow the van* a Music Hall number?" asked Alice.

"Yeah," said Hen. "The one that goes, 'I dillied and dallied'?"

Remarkably, they soon came up with a couple more. Tom knew the chorus of *After the ball* and Hen suggested *You are my honeysuckle*. It turned out that Tom was actually a pretty good singer. He got them learning the chorus words of *After the ball* and then they were all singing away and having a great time.

Alice felt it first. She kept singing as she grabbed Tom's hand and... it happened. They both flipped.

Inside the fifth, they held on to each other, firmly. Then Hen and Nadia appeared. They worked the slope until they met up. But there was no Roxanne.

"Roxanne?" communicated Alice.

"We can't leave her!" interacted Nadia. "No way."

"But this is our chance!" argued Alice.

"No. Not without Rox!" Nadia tried to let go of Hen to make towards the vortex, but Hen held on.

"Wait, Nadia," he telegraphed – they were all drifting dangerously close to the whirlpool, now.

"She's right," sent Tom, squeezing Alice's hand. "We can't leave Roxanne."

Alice glanced up towards the horizon – a ridge over which her parents and family were waiting for her. But it was too late. She knew they wouldn't make it. And she knew, too, that she couldn't do it. How could she live with herself if she deserted Roxanne – or any of them? And Tom was already following Nadia back to the vortex. Alice held Tom's hand and they re-entered together.

"Where the hell were you?" demanded Alice of Roxanne as they landed in a heap on the floor in front of her. "Why didn't you join us?"

"I... I... I wasn't ready. I didn't expect it," Roxanne explained.

"Don't you *want* to go back?" Alice spoke too strongly and tears came into Roxanne's eyes.

"Yes. One day," she sighed, drying her eyes. "But... look

next time it happens. Next time just keep going. Don't worry about me."

"Nah. There ain't no way we're leaving you!" stated Nadia, emphatically.

"Roxanne, we can't leave you," said Hen, calmly. "We can't turn the clock back. I guess you can't go back to where you were – not now, not with all that's happening."

"Don't even think about it, Rox," said Tom, giving her a hug. "You belong with us. Right? We all go or none of us goes."

Alice felt bad. She so wanted to get home. None of the others had quite what she had back there; none of them had a brother or sister. But she mustn't be selfish. And, there was something – a bond, especially with Tom. "Sorry, Rox," she said. "I didn't mean to be cross. That was unkind... I wouldn't leave you. I couldn't leave anyone. We belong together – all of us." Alice joined in the hugs.

Hen cleared his throat and struck up a business tone. "Right. Back to the music."

"We need a name," reckoned Tom. "A group needs a name."

"You're right," agreed Nadia. "How about 'The Five Dimensions'. I mean it's true. We're 5D survivors, ain't we?"

"I like it," smiled Tom.

Hen grinned his approval and struck up a note. *"The honeysuckle and the bee.* You sing it to Roxanne, Tom. Rox's got the best voice to sing with you."

"Yeah," said Nadia, "Take her hand – perform it. She's your honeysuckle, got it?"

"And I'm the bee?" laughed Tom.

"Yeah. It's kinda romantic, innit?" laughed Nadia, with mock disgust.

Tom was amazing. He even amazed himself. He'd only once before got a chance to perform. He had never been in the drama group at school.

25

The next morning they listened to the radio while having a late breakfast. It was The Voice's weekly morning radio play. Most of the time, their hostess told them, it was blatant propaganda.

But as they listened, she became quite animated. When the play's leading man gave some flowers to the leading lady, the lady said how much she adored roses – especially the yellow ones. That was it! Apparently, that was a coded communication for the Streatham MPC group.

"That was a message for us!" declared their hostess. "It's blooming amazing! The characters are giving coded messages of encouragement. I bet it's *all* a load of information to our MPC cells across the country. Absolutely amazing. We've infiltrated The Voice and they don't even realise it! Things're really warming up."

The teenagers were gobsmacked. It was fantastic watching the excitement of this woman and knowing their particular part in it. Of course, they couldn't let on; she had no idea how the messages had got into the play.

"Whoever pulled that off was absolutely brilliant!" she

said. Tom and Hen daren't look at one another.

"Yes, brilliant," repeated Hen. "Unless you knew, you wouldn't have the faintest idea of what all this means."

"I can't imagine how it got into the system at The Voice!" exclaimed the woman. "One day we might even be using The Voice – state media itself! – to tell all the cells when to act in unison. Then, at last, the régime will fall."

The programme continued uninterrupted. It seemed the fascist authorities hadn't a clue what was happening. They had not guessed the drugs in the élite dining hall was a ruse to keep the head of propaganda out of his office. And those who had written the original script – the one Hen had stolen – had all been prevented from going back to work; some of them were probably incarcerated already.

At that moment, Alice realised the significance of what they had done. It was a strange feeling. She recalled learning about agents doing really important work behind enemy lines in the Second World War. They helped to win the war but their contributions were not known until decades later – if ever. Some of them had even put up with people saying they were lazy or that they were cowards and stuff but they weren't ever allowed to let on. Those people would be gutted to know that, in this parallel world, the Nazis had won! But the people here had not given up – the battle had continued, decade after decade. The resistance had not ever gone away – and this lady was one of them. Alice caught something of the thrill that, at last, cracks were beginning to show. Then she remembered that all of what the Movement for Peaceful Change had achieved that day had probably been months in the planning and they had entrusted the whole execution to them. An alarming thought! *What if we had mucked up? I'm glad I didn't know just how important this was at the time!* Alice told herself.

Alice spoke quietly to their host. "You're taking a big risk having us here," she said, solemnly. "I mean to trust us and all that."

"I'm pretty good at knowing who I can trust," said the woman. "It's *you* I worry about. You, young lady, say everything in your face. You're not natural at hiding things, are you?"

"I was always brought up to know that lying was wrong," responded Alice, ruefully. "Mum and Dad taught me that it was one thing to do something wrong but far worse to lie about it. I don't do lying easily."

"You're going to have to get better at it here," chirped Roxanne.

"I know! I know!" Alice was getting a bit tetchy at being told once again that she was too open. "I'm trying!... But what am I going to do? We are going on the *stage*. I'll be in full view! That's, like, stupid."

"Best place," smiled the woman. "If you're going to stand out you might as well do it properly. Everyone has to earn a living – especially a few homeless young people. I've no idea how you got here and I've no idea what you're up to – if anything. All I know is that you need a place to stay and that you have to come up with an act by this afternoon... How's it coming on?"

"We're working on it," said Hen. "Does the Astoria have a piano?"

"Of course. It even has an organ. Can you play?"

"The piano – a bit. Never tried an organ... anyway, I can only remember very little – I'm not good at just playing what someone sings to me."

"They must have some sheet music," thought the woman. "Just ask when you get there."

26

They were glad to step inside the lobby of the Astoria – wearing the rather heavy clothing, it was pretty hot in the sunshine. Back home, Alice would definitely be in her shorts and sleeveless top rather than a three-quarter length flannel skirt and dull-coloured, long-sleeved thick linen blouse. But it suited the purpose – no one gave her a second glance. Even Nadia blended in despite her black skin – you couldn't see much of it.

The lobby of the theatre was decorated with a shabby set of murals that had seen better days. In places, they had been painted over but you could still make out some sort of desert palm trees and a river that looked like it was meant to be ancient Egypt. They were greeted by the most ornately dressed man they had seen in Nazi London. In a bottle-green velvet waistcoat, he looked positively theatrical. And when he spoke, he sounded decidedly weird.

"My darlings," he began. "Are you the troupe that we have been waiting for to light up the dull evenings of the populace? Not that I am promising many of the populace – although I am always longing for the glories of the past. It could be that you are what we need to get them flocking in, eh?"

"Hello. We call ourselves the Five Dimensions," said Hen, extending a hand.

"Ah. *Brilliant*. I *love* it; the play on the 'i' - five, dime - love it! Just so long as you stay *alive*, *revive* our fortunes and don't take a *dive*, eh?" He chuckled at his own joke.

Hen forced a laugh. The others just stared.

"Love me little joke?" continued the man, disappointed at the response. "Bit of a clown really. Wanted to do stand up but got booed off. So I manage a whole theatre instead... I say 'theatre'" he added, looking glum. "Ninety per cent of the time it's a cinema where we show 'improving' films. But, today, *what ho!* We have *five live dimensions* to perform! What's your act?"

"We do Old Time Music Hall," said Hen. The manager clapped his hands.

"Oh. *Wonderful*. Get them all singing. I *love* audience participation!"

"But we have a small problem," continued Hen. "We're, actually, completely under-rehearsed and... er... I have not been able to bring my sheet music – for the, er, piano... You have a piano, I hear."

"We do! *We do!*... Can't remember when it was last tuned

though... come to think of it, I can't remember when it was last played. But music for it we have in abundance! This is *wonderful*, so wonderful! The dust is *flying* in the old Astoria. Come in! *Come in!* "

He led them through into the auditorium. It was huge. The stalls cascaded down towards a high stage and above them they could make out several tiers of seats that formed the circles. As they descended towards the stage, Alice looked back and studied the banks of seats in amazement. The manager caught her expression.

"Yes. Big, isn't it? Three thousand seats or thereabouts. Never filled them in my time."

The ceiling was all latticework and there were more Egyptian scenes – all in dire need of restoration. Clearly, nothing had been done for decades; it spoke loudly of former glories.

"Opened in 1930 – you have come to help us celebrate our opening on 30th June that year," smiled the man. "Just mind you *pack 'em in*, eh?"

"When are we to... er...? I mean, if we pass our audition?" asked Hen.

"Why tonight, young man. We will put your act on in between the two films. That way you've got an audience. Can't afford to advertise..." he tried to give a jolly smile. "Come.

Come, let me introduce you to the old joanna!" And he toddled off down the remainder of the aisle and up a flight of steps onto the stage. The young people followed him into one of the wings and behind a large canvass movie screen. Behind it, the stage was enormous. In the far corner was a grand piano under a dust sheet which the manager swept off with a flourish. Clouds of dust rose into the air causing Alice to sneeze. The man didn't seem to notice, however.

Hen raised the keyboard lid. It would have been a magnificent instrument in its day. He tried a chord and winced. The manager winced even more. Hen sat down and ran through a scale in C major. It had been a while and Hen would need a lot of practice. But the manager did not hear Hen's lack of fluency – only the badly tuned instrument.

"No!" he gulped. "No. Damn the expense – got to get you tuned up, madam!" He turned to the Five Dimensions and commanded, "Practice if you will, practice..." and mumbled, "Leave this to me!" and disappeared off the stage.

Hen tried playing *My Old Man* but it was awful. "I am playing some wrong notes – or, at least, I think I am. But this piano is impossible."

"I think he's gone to find someone to tune it," said Roxanne.

"Needs it," grunted Tom. "I can't sing to that."

144

"*A cappella?*" asked Hen.

Tom shook his head. "No way."

Just then a young woman in a short, bouncy dress, which made her look like a doll, came onto the stage. "Mr Pottinger says to show you the music," she announced, prettily. "It's this way."

She led them towards what must once have been dressing rooms. Through half-opened doors, Alice spotted stacked furniture, stage props of all descriptions, a magician's chest and a Punch and Judy booth as well as a myriad of smaller things. In one of the rooms, several large cupboards stood against the far wall. The doll opened one of them. It was fitted with shelves containing stacks and stacks of sheet music.

Where to begin? thought Alice.

The girl smiled. "Mr Pottinger says, 'Do you want tea?' I can make you a nice cup of tea."

Alice could think of nothing better – the dust was really getting to her.

"Yes. Thanks," she said. They all wanted tea. Hen looked through a pile of music – it all appeared to be classical. "Where do we begin?" asked Alice.

"No idea," said Hen.

"Better pray," suggested Roxanne.

Nadia had to say something. "You've really got it bad,

ain't you? This praying thing."

"Never did no harm," said Roxanne, defensively. "And these people believe in it."

"That's because they're desperate," contributed Alice.

"Yeah. So are we if we're on tonight," muttered Roxanne.

"And I'm not singing without a piano," asserted Tom.

"OK," began Nadia, loudly. "Let's pray..." and then added, bluntly, "God, show us where to find the music Hen needs!"

"That's a bit... brutal," ventured Alice. "I mean a bit bossy... to God. I mean... if He exists... And you're supposed to end with 'Amen'."

Nadia was not going to be cowed. "Yeah? But God, *if* He's listening, is going to have to put up with me talking the way I would to anyone else. I wasn't rude. That's *me* being *me*... and if God don't like it, He can stuff it, OK?... 'God, help us to find the effing music. Amen.'"

"Nadia!" exclaimed Alice. "That *was* rude!"

"Sorry God!" sang Nadia. Roxanne began to giggle.

"Hey you guys," said Hen. "I think I've found what we're looking for! Look, all this pile is Old Time Music Hall. '*Come into the garden, Maud*', '*After the ball is over*', '*You are my honeysuckle*'. And there's loads more." Hen continued to dust off more sheets. "And with all the words! Guys, I reckon we've hit gold!"

"Alleluia!" chanted Nadia.

"I told you praying works!" laughed Roxanne.

"That's why I said 'Alleluia', innit?"

"Impressive," said Tom.

"Right," urged Hen, "let's get working on this."

The doll returned with a tray of tea. "Mr Pottinger has got a bloke coming to put the piana right," she announced. "Mr Pottinger says if you don't mind practising without her while she's getting tuned. He says you can do it in your dressing room if it's big enough. Have you found what you want here?"

"Yes. I think so," said Hen. "Here, you and Roxanne take the '*You are my honeysuckle*' and get working on it. I'll carry on here and see what else there is."

The girl carried the tray, followed by Tom, Roxanne and Alice, to a cleaner-looking room with a row of seats facing a line of mirrors across dressing tables. She put the tray down. "This place was for the chorus girls," she explained. "About time it got used... Lav's through there." She pointed to a door bearing the title, 'Lavatories' and an arrow. "Don't use the gents – it don't work. Sorry about the mirrors. Place hasn't been used for three months. I don't get to clean it much."

"Are you the cleaner?" asked Tom.

"Yeah. Cleaner, usherette, secretary, tea-maker, general

dog's body. There's only me and Mrs Pottinger who work here – apart from Mr Pottinger."

"It must be hard work when this place is full," ventured Tom.

"Full! You're kidding me. It's never anywhere near full. Never get more than a couple a dozen. Never been anyone upstairs in the circles as long as I have been coming here – since I was a kid. Upstairs is so full of spiders and things that eat them, I wouldn't dare go up there."

Clutching some more music, Hen and Nadia joined them. They heard the sound of a piano being tuned.

"You're some'ut, ain't you?" gushed the doll. "Must be if he's got a tuner in so quick. Mr Pottinger likes the look of you... And so do I!" She reddened, turned and was off, disappearing through the door like the fair-weather girl on a barometer.

"We're not going to flip here, are we?" asked Alice, only half-rhetorically.

"Guess we can't," sighed Tom. "It would be awful if we just vanished after 'Mr Pottinger' has gone to the expense of getting the piano tuned."

"Not as bad as making a fool of ourselves trying to sing," reasoned Alice.

"We won't," said Tom. "I reckon we can do something... there'll not be many people, anyhow."

"If God's found us the music," affirmed Roxanne. "I guess we can keep praying that He will help us to perform it."

"He'd better!" said Nadia. "Or He's going to get a piece of my mind!" Alice couldn't help laughing at her. She liked the refreshing way Nadia spoke of God. Her mum and dad told her to be truthful but around where she lived, people seemed to come over all different when they went to church – they put on a kind of church face. The weddings and christenings she'd been to had all been dressed up affairs and people were quiet and shushed their children. She'd hated going to church as a child because you had to be on your best behaviour. And the place was big and echoey and cold... And, worse than anything, she had believed that God had been watching her there – in *His* house – and would get angry with her if she wasn't good. She had learned God had a special word for bad things: sins. And you always felt like a sinner, even if you couldn't think of anything you had done wrong.

But Nadia would say that that was all crap. She wasn't fazed by the idea of God. If He existed, He would have to accept her as she was, "or stuff it."

As Tom and Roxanne sorted out how they would tackle their song, Alice drifted on thinking. *In one way, Nadia's, like, rather ordinary. She's what Mum would call 'working class' but she's deep. There're things going on there that I don't know.* Then Alice remembered the conversation when Nadia had said she wasn't ready to hear something. *I wonder what Nadia was talking about when she said that? That girl's got such a secret side. Sometimes she makes me feel like I'm still a little girl... And Roxanne? She has, like, loads more street sense than me...* And at that moment Alice began to feel small – and on the outside. She wanted so much to go home. And she knew it. *I don't belong here, do I? They keep saying they wouldn't flip without Roxanne – or Nadia – but I bet they wouldn't miss me if I went.*

Alice shook herself and told herself to stop thinking like that; she mustn't take a "poor-little-me" attitude. After all, she was a 400-metre champion... or had been before the flipping began. And her friends told her she wasn't bad looking... well, before she had had all her hair hacked off.

27

Tom and Roxanne took their copies of *You are my honeysuckle* and Tom sang a couple of notes until he got one about right on which to start. He sang the first verse as best he could and then Roxanne joined him in the chorus. Hen and Nadia had a go as Tom was in the middle of the second verse.

"OK," said Hen, when they had finished singing the chorus for a second time. "That's great. But I reckon we should all join in the chorus, and Tom and Roxanne, you have to *act it* and sing it as if you mean it. Look each other in the eyes. If you do it right, that'll cover up a heap of other stuff."

They went through it a couple more times. It transpired that Tom was not bad at all. And Roxanne could certainly act. They looked into each other's eyes and pretended to be in love. *Roxanne can be quite the seductress when she tries*, noted Alice.

What happened next took Alice by surprise. Over the course of the third rehearsal, she went – felt – kind of funny inside. She became all hot and panicky... and angry. She hoped her revealing face wasn't betraying what was going on inside her. She knew what had brought it on – it was when

Roxanne looked all coy at Tom like that. *Am I jealous?!* she thought. She'd never laid claim to Tom. They were just friends, right? Always had been, even when Prof W thought they were having it off with each other. But now, with Roxanne looking at him like that and him singing, "I'd like to sip the honey sweet from those red lips" she felt, like... *If Tom's going to sing that yucky stuff to anyone, it should be me!* She thought of suggesting – volunteering – to do it instead but she knew she couldn't do it like Roxanne. She couldn't act like that – look like some – what was her name? – Cleopatra, in that ancient Egyptian setting.

Hen applauded. This was coming together well.

"Alice," he said, "you look too sad. You must look like you're enjoying it... like last night. You got into it and you flipped."

"But we ain't flipping tonight," affirmed, Roxanne. "It wouldn't be fair on Mr Pottinger. I like him."

"But you *would* say that!" blurted Alice, angrily. "*You* like it here – in this London. You *never* liked it on our side. It's not fair for *you* to keep us here!" Then she burst into tears.

"I... I told you!" returned Roxanne, forcefully. "I *told* you not to stay here for me. I never asked you to stay. If you can get away. Go! Don't mind me."

Nadia stepped in; she was upset. "We ain't going

nowhere," she stated, bluntly. "Alice you told me not to be rude to God. But you've just been horrible to Rox!"

Alice crumpled into a chair. Tears streamed down her face. Then Tom knelt beside her and took her hand. "I think I know where this is coming from," he said, kindly and softly. "Of all of us you fit least into this London. You hate pretending. You don't like acting and this is all an act – the acting is an act. But Roxanne has found a way of helping people – something she never knew back home. You can't blame her for wanting to feel useful... More than useful. We were all amazing yesterday at the broadcasting place, weren't we? Including you. Can we just go with the flow – for now? We're not going to be here forever. I promise. But we can't leave Rox at the moment. And these people are amazing, too. We've helped once; maybe we can help them again. If nothing else happens, we've cheered up that Mr Pottinger."

Alice looked up, tears were streaming down her cheeks; Tom just took her in his strong arms. He'd never done that before – not like that. It was the first time anyone had properly cuddled her since she had said goodbye to her parents all those months ago. She clung to him. She hadn't realised just how much she needed to be held. Hen beckoned to the others and soon they were all in a group hug.

Tom gave Alice a handkerchief. She blew her nose and looked up. She saw Roxanne looking at her full of care.

"S... sorry, Rox," she said. "I didn't mean to be cruel. That was awful."

Roxanne gave her arm a squeeze. "That's OK," she said, "I understand. I really do. I'm not staying here forever, you know. I have to go back sometime. But, it's just, that these people have been so kind. I'm sorry I got cross with you."

"No... No, it's me. I was just feeling so crap all of a sudden." Alice sniffed and Tom passed her a box of tissues from the table. He looked at her and in his eyes, there was genuine care – he wasn't pretending.

They heard a smart tap on the door.

"All right to come in?" It was the manager. "The jolly old joana's back to her best," he announced, with a broad smile.

"Thanks," said Hen. "OK. Let's have a go at that song on the piano. If that's all right now, sir...?"

"Certainly. Be my guest," Mr Pottinger beamed. "Delighted."

The manager was more than delighted when he heard them. Tom and Roxanne acted like pros and the chorus was resounding as Hen joined in from the piano.

"Sorry, no mike," shrugged Mr Pottinger. "Sounds awful to say so in this day and age but there it is. You'll have to project as best you can. I'll try and get people to sit as close as possible but with the films and all, they tend to scatter about.

But you're going to be a riot. I just know it!" He clapped his hands together and gave them a broad smile. "Now, costumes. I am right in thinking you lack costumes?"

"We've nothing but what we're wearing," muttered Hen.

"Right, follow me!" The manager took them beneath the stage where there were racks upon racks of theatre costumes for both sexes and in every size. There was stuff that glittered and stuff that looked formal and skimpy stuff that Alice was amazed to see.

"Now then! Um... Music Hall. Morning suits for the gentlemen, I would say. Have a look in this row. Dicky bows somewhere in the draws – they're all labelled. Ladies, cocktail dresses? No, you're too young... I know: 'Alice' gowns. They come in all colours not just blue. Over here!"

He took them to a rack of full dresses with capacious frilly underskirts to go with them. "And wigs! Let me see. I think *you*," he took Alice by the hand, "would look absolutely adorable in long blonde hair... Here we are! Just your colour!" he exclaimed and presented Alice with a blonde wig that was, for all the world, exactly like her own hair that she had had to have cut off only days before. It did the trick. Alice smiled her broadest smile.

"Thank you, Mr Pottinger," she said, graciously, and put her arms around his corpulent figure.

"Yes. Yes..." he sang, embarrassed by Alice's touch. "G... Glad you like it!"

So, thought Alice, I get to pretend to be me! She put the wig on and checked herself in a mirror.

"Yes," smiled Tom, laughing. "You look *exactly* right. It suits you. I wonder why?"

"Thanks, Tom. So I get to resemble something like me. That's quite lucky, I guess." She looked up at him. "Thanks," she said, with deep sincerity.

"For what?" asked Tom.

"Being so patient with me."

"That's easy," he said. "No sweat. Glad you're feeling more like you."

Soon all five were decked in the most gorgeous clothes. Mr Pottinger was, "Delighted!"

"What about the audition?" asked Hen. "You've given us all this – got the piano right. But we were supposed to come for an audition."

"Of course you're hired!" replied the manager. "I'll get Sallyanne to bring you more tea, so you keep practising. Then we can get in some fish and chips – what do you say?"

"Great," grinned Nadia.

"Then you will be all set to come on for, say, twenty minutes at 8.30 after the end of the supporting film," explained the manager. "Get them in the mood for the rather dull feature film of how Hitler gained power in Germany in the 1920s and 30s. It's not well acted in my opinion but don't tell anyone I told you that." He winked and his eyes twinkled. "With the radio only playing military music these days, we might get a better turn out."

"Military music?" asked Hen.

"Yes. And recorded speeches from the prime minister. The Voice is suspended – seems the station has been the victim of some attack. An announcer keeps coming on to say that normal service will be resumed as soon as possible. If we're in luck, that won't be until after your performance, eh?"

29

After the fish and chips, which had cheered them all up enormously, the five young people were ready to perform. None of them had tasted fish and chips like that since before they had entered the Winterford. Why do fish and chips cooked in a shop and wrapped up in paper taste so different from anything cooked in a home kitchen?

Looking out at the audience from a side door, Hen counted just fifteen people, excluding Mr and Mrs Pottinger and Sallyanne sitting at the rear of the stalls. After a short break during which Sallyanne managed to sell a couple of bags of sweets, Mr Pottinger mounted the steps to the stage and introduced the half-time act. He urged the audience to group closer together to enable them to participate better. No one moved.

After the first song – *My Old Man* – the troupe were encouraged when half a dozen came closer. By the time they had got to the chorus a second time – *I dillied and dallied, and dallied and dillied...* – there were several people all joining in quite audibly.

After the song ended, one man stood and applauded. He

yelled, "Encore! Encore!".

Hen looked at his troupe and struck up again with the chorus. This time, even the few sitting at the back stood and joined in.

When Hen began playing *God be with you,* the same man stood immediately and bowed his head as they sang. They noticed he had tears rolling down his face by the time they had finished.

The Five Dimensions took a final bow and scampered off.

After that, the main feature started showing and Mr Pottinger came into the dressing room and congratulated them. "*Wonderful,* my darlings. *Wonderful!* " he shook their hands. "I'm sorry there's no champagne but you would have it if I had any."

"Thanks, Mr Pottinger," said Roxanne.

"*Tomorrow!* I'll see you tomorrow. I'll be here anytime from two o'clock if you want to do some more rehearsing."

"Yes, of course," said Hen. "It was all good fun and you have been so nice to us... but," he added, in quieter tones, "you will understand what I mean when we say we have to 'go with the flow' so we can't promise anything."

"Of course, of course... but let's hope the flow is in the direction of the Astoria!"

It was. Transmissions appeared to have got back to normal at The Voice – although rumour had it that a lot of people had disappeared and the place had been turned into a veritable fortress. Alice thought of the dragon and hoped she had been able to remain undercover. She was thinking of the woman when she realised that if the dragon was being interrogated she might be forced to talk about her three two-day apprentices. Alice shuddered but there was nothing they could do. Anyway, the dragon would have no idea where they were.

They turned up at the Astoria with their new personae established – they even had new fake ID cards issued by the Association of Professional Entertainers.

"Ah, I see you are members of APE!" declared Mr Pottinger. "That's excellent. Being an APE allows you to behave a little unusually... out of the ordinary... which, indeed you are! Extraordinary! I am so looking forward to seeing you perform again," he chortled.

Hen found another song that had been immensely popular in the Music Halls: *Come into the garden Maud*. "It's a bit of a challenge," he said. "Lot's of words, Tom, but it will be the icing on the cake."

"You've really got the bug, haven't you?" laughed Tom.

"Yes. I must say that I am enjoying playing again."

"Let's have a look at it, then," said Tom.

Tom was one of those lucky people who could learn lines extremely fast and it was coming together well when he said, "I reckon Alice would make an ideal Maud in her shy and coy mode. It's a non-singing part, of course."

"Yeah, You'd be perfect," beamed Roxanne.

"Do it," commanded Nadia.

Alice didn't want Roxanne to take yet another part in which she played up to Tom, so she readily agreed.

That evening things were different. To everyone's amazement, people arrived in numbers. Whole families – young and old – but lots of people Alice's grandparents' age poured through the doors. Sallyanne was struggling to issue the tickets and Mr Pottinger had to do the ushering himself. He lost count of the number of people but it was well in excess of a hundred – and they all wanted to sit at the front. It was quite clear they had not come for the film.

30

On the third evening, it was amazing. A huge queue snaked outside the theatre, around the corner and up Pendennis Road. The Five Dimensions had to act as ushers inside the theatre as Mr and Mrs Pottinger and Sallyanne battled to issue the tickets as fast as they could.

As the first film was being projected, Mr Pottinger bounced into the dressing room. He was excited. But he was also nervous.

"They've all come for you," he declared, "you're too good. The word has got around fast." Then he smiled, "The truth is, you bring a dose of fresh air that we haven't known in decades. We British are not naturally morose but these days you can even be arrested for smiling in the street. People know this is their only chance… And I'm afraid you'll have to scarper tomorrow – you're attracting far too much attention. But tonight, my darlings, give us all what we so long for, eh!" He clapped Hen on the back and put his arm around Tom's shoulders.

The applause was encouraging from the moment they appeared on stage. Nadia didn't have to work hard at getting them to join in. It was during the *My Old Man* chorus that two stern looking men in BUF black appeared at the back of the auditorium but, hidden as they were in the shadows, the Five Dimensions did not see them.

Alice was nervous when they came to the Maud song. She stood timidly pretending to look over a hardboard gate – which Mr Pottinger had come up with – when Tom appeared from behind it. As the opening strains began, Alice was meant to retreat a bit and do her coy thing and her nerves only added to the performance. Tom entreated her from over the gate. "Come into the garden, Maud," he sang, followed by a lot of other words that Alice, in her panic, didn't take in. They were all meant to entice her into the "garden".

Eventually, Tom joined her on her side of the gate, took her hand and looked down at her. She met his soft gaze. The song ended but he kept looking into her eyes. Hen continued to play. The scene that followed hadn't been planned. What Alice saw in those blue eyes was so genuine. She didn't know what made her do it. Keeping her eyes on his, she raised her face and leaned forward on tiptoe. The next thing she was aware of was their lips had met and Tom was kissing her.

It was the deafening whoops from the audience that broke the spell. Nadia and Roxanne stood aghast but Hen launched straight into *God be with you* and that covered Alice's confusion. She had just kissed Tom for the first time *in front of hundreds of people!* It was a kiss softer and gentler than she had ever imagined a kiss could be – just amazing. If Tom hadn't held her waist, she was sure her knees would have given way! *Alice,* she told herself, as they sang the finale, *that was unbelievably daft.* But Tom had meant it, too! That was the amazing thing. She didn't regret it but what would the others think? What would they say? How could she explain it? She hoped Tom would have the words.

But, as soon as they took their bow and left the stage, Sallyanne was in the wings. Instead of congratulating them, she spoke urgently with a look of fear in her eyes. "You must leave – immediately!" she ordered. "Straight out the stage door. There is a car."

"But we need to change," said Hen.

"No. No time. Your belongings are already in the car. You must leave as you are. The Sestapo are coming backstage as we speak. Go!" She thrust a few notes into Hen's hand. "Your wages. Go!" and then turned. They could hear Mr Pottinger addressing the audience. He was announcing the National Anthem. As they got to the stage door into Pendennis Road they heard the strains of the military music.

"He's delaying them," explained Roxanne. "No one can ignore the National Anthem."

"This is *Sound* of flipping *Music,*" muttered Nadia, "only for real! It ain't so romantic when it's, like, actually happening. Von Trapp - Von Crap more like!... And now it's turned into blooming Cinderella - it seems our carriage awaits."

A large car stood in front of them with its doors open and engine running. The girls and Tom piled into the back seat leaving Hen to take the seat next to the driver. The car drove off even before they could get the doors closed. Four hot bodies sorted themselves into three rear seats. As the car swung around a corner, Tom put his hands onto Alice's waist, lifted her onto his lap and held her tight.

"You two!" screamed Roxanne, "I like it!"

"Oh, it's been going on for ages," grunted Nadia. "Even Prof W thought they were at it."

"But we weren't!" protested Alice.

"You were," laughed Nadia, "You just didn't know it."

"Where are we going?" asked Hen of the driver. They had weaved through several back streets and were now on a more major road.

"You'll see. If we're followed, orders are to dump you... Here." He tossed a small box into Hen's lap. "Cyanide. Chew on this if you don't want to be interrogated... Pass them around."

Hen opened the box, took out a capsule and passed the box into the back seat. All thought of the amazing performance, the delighted audience and Tom and Alice's kiss vanished; it was like being dropped into a freezing bath.

The driver kept checking his mirrors and eventually pulled into a side road and stopped. Were they being dumped? Was this it?

"Get into that car in front," ordered the driver. "Take your stuff out of the boot. What are you waiting for? Go!"

Hen swung his door open and pulled open the back door before dragging a bag out of the boot. Alice slipped off Tom's knee while Nadia and Roxanne got out the driver's side of the vehicle. They each grabbed a carpet bag and stepped onto the pavement. As soon as the boot slammed shut the driver was off. The rear of the car in front opened for them as if by magic and they hoisted their bags into it. It was a bigger car and had three rows of seats. This driver seemed more relaxed. He was in no hurry to pull away but watched his mirror to see if any official car seemed to be following the first. No cars passed them at all. He pulled out and regained the main road. It appeared that the cyanide would not be necessary for the moment at least. Alice shuddered as she felt the capsule against her skin – she had pushed it into her bra. She wondered if it would melt. Could cyanide poison you through your skin?

After a quarter of an hour, they had begun to leave the

built-up area and soon they were on a country road with few cars. It became dark and the stars came out and the car pulled into a quiet lay-by.

"Change here," said the driver. "You are going on an ocean liner as the entertainment. Keep your theatre clothes safe."

As Alice took off her wig it seemed strange. The long hair was her, the short was not. She stowed it carefully. She put the poison capsule in the bottom of the bag; if she was caught she knew she wouldn't be brave enough to take it – she would take her chances. She noticed that Nadia did the same but Roxanne put hers into a pocket in her knickers. Seeing Alice watching her, Roxanne announced, "I never got used to not wearing trousers, so I made pockets in all my undies – not that I got to put much into them except... except this. She pulled out a folded banknote. "Never know when you might need some dosh." Roxanne laughed. Now she had a suicide pill to keep the note company and it was clear that she would use it. Alice wondered whether that was because Roxanne was braver or more scared than her because she was a bit more aware of what the Nazis did.

Now back in their day clothes – and Alice feeling distinctly less attractive – they recommenced their journey. It was long and they all fell asleep.

31

They were entering the outskirts of a city as the sun rose. The driver told them it was Southampton.

"I am to leave you outside the railway station. Then you have to make your way to the Oswald Mosley Terminal and find the *SS United States*. They are expecting you on board this morning. They sail tomorrow for New York."

"New York?!" exclaimed Nadia.

"As in America?" marvelled Alice, stunned.

"As in America," echoed the driver. "You kids aren't safe here."

"Makes logical sense," observed Hen, calmly.

"Who's buying the tickets?" Roxanne wanted to know.

"No one. You are to work your passage. You're going as entertainers. Here's a letter of introduction. You are to ask for a Mr Springer... don't worry, it isn't his real name."

"Thanks," said Hen. "We are most obliged—"

Roxanne interrupted him. "It's not just about looking after us, is it? We're a liability. The fact is we know too much and too many people."

"Yes." concurred the driver. "You were too blooming good in the entertainment industry and attracted far too much attention. Now you're on their radar, you'll serve the cause better out of the way. They nearly got you at the theatre."

"I hope nothing's happened to the Pottingers and Sallyanne," murmured Alice, feeling troubled.

The driver pulled into a taxi rank outside Southampton Central Station. They got out and retrieved their bags from the back, the driver wished them luck and then pulled away.

They stood looking around them. They had no idea which way to go for the docks so Hen approached a taxi driver.

"Excuse me. Can you tell us which way to go for the docks?"

"Docks? Which dock? What ship are you looking for?"

"The Oswald Mosley terminal. The SS *United States*."

"That way. Half a mile. Hop in."

"We have little—"

"How much?" asked Roxanne. The man surveyed them.

"For you, nothing. Get in. My missus tells me I'll never be rich. But you're clearly worse off than me. You got jobs?"

"We're a troupe of entertainers," answered Hen.

"Really poor then. When you get famous and fabulously rich in Hollywood you can pay me."

They were outside the dock building within three minutes. The *SS United States* was huge. The dark blue hull and brilliant white superstructure towered above them.

Hen thanked the taxi driver. Then he remembered the notes that Sallyanne had given him as they had left the Astoria; he'd quite forgotten them. He fished one out. "Here," he said, giving the man a note. "I'd forgotten I had this."

The man protested and refused to take it.

"No," Hen used his best grown-up voice. "We're off to New York. We can't spend it there. It's yours."

"Well," said the taxi driver. "I always told the missus that it pays to be generous. You kids look after yourselves and I hope that one day you *will* make it in Hollywood. I'll say a prayer for you."

"Thanks," said Roxanne, "We'll need it."

As they approached the entrance, a policeman armed with an assault rifle intercepted their path.

"ID," he ordered.

They set down their bags on the pavement and searched out their ID cards. The policeman scrutinised them and their faces. Then seemed satisfied.

"Keep them visible around here in future," he commanded. "Where are you going?"

"We have a position on the *SS United States*," stated Hen.

"We're a troupe of entertainers."

"What do you do?"

"Sing," said Hen. "Or at least they do. I play the piano."

The policeman ordered Alice to open her bag. Holding his rifle in his right hand, he rummaged among Alice's stage costume with his left and came out with the wig." He snorted. Clearly, the contents of the bag confirmed Hen's explanation. The policeman dismissed them, leaving Alice to repack her bag.

"Charming," said Nadia, after the man had turned his attention to a petrified-looking elderly couple.

"Charm. That's one thing you can guarantee they have not got," spat Roxanne.

"With a bit of luck, that'll be the last time we meet such a man before we get on board," said Hen.

Roxanne grimaced. "You wanna bet?"

Inside the terminal, they were approached by a large man in a different kind of uniform. It looked nautical. "You got your tickets?" he asked in a distinctive North American accent, which sounded incredibly laid back after the policeman. Hen produced the letter. The man smiled – actually smiled.

"You'll find Mr Springer in that office over there. The purser's office."

They looked in the direction in which he was pointing and

saw an A-board with the words "Purser's Office." Hen thanked the gentleman. "Thank you, sir." They dragged their bags over to the office doorway. There was a short queue in front of a reception desk attended by a neat woman in a formal two-piece suit. Hen gave the letter to Roxanne. "Do you want to go in while we wait here by the bags?" He had become aware that since the formation of the troupe he had become the *de facto* leader and voice. But Roxanne had more experience and it should be she who took them through.

"Me?" she questioned.

"You can do this better than I can – you're the one with the experience," he explained. "I think I have become caught up in the ways of this sexist society. Forgive me."

"It's probably different in America," said Tom. "And that ship *is* America."

"Let's hope it is," sighed Alice. "But, I've been thinking. Once we're on board, we're never going to be able to flip back to our Britain. If we're in the middle of the Atlantic we daren't cross the horizon in the fifth – we might end up in the sea and drown."

"Getting back to England from New York in our world, though, ain't going to be that hard," remarked Nadia. "There're dozens of planes every day – your mum and dad will buy you a ticket for sure. And you heard what that man said. We can't stay here, they're on to us. There'll be a warrant out for us."

"They aren't watching this port yet, or else that policeman would have done for us," reasoned Tom.

"Not so far," grunted Roxanne, flatly. "Give me that letter. Five young people together are too obvious. The sooner we are on board and 'in America', the better." She entered the office and joined the queue.

The woman took the letter, read the address and smiled. She lifted a receiver on her desk and dialled a number and spoke in an American accent."Mr Springer'll be right over. Just wait by that door. She sounded just like Jennifer Lawrence.

32

Mr Springer was typically Hollywood – and the Entertainment Director aboard the *SS United States*. He opened the letter and read it.

"I can't say just how glad I am to see you," he began, in what definitely sounded like a West Coast accent. Alice got a whiff of Katie Perry. "In your costumes you'll look absolutely fabulous. What a rarity! So unusual to find teenagers with initiative in this country. And what wonderful reviews... I don't suppose you have passports?" They showed their IDs. "No, I mean passports with visas to enter the US?" Roxanne shook her head. "Never you mind. I shall officially take you on a round trip. That way I can tick all the company's boxes. But don't worry, once you're in New York you can claim asylum; that's the way it works. I've never come across anyone being refused it." And then he talked and talked and talked as he led them through another door and up a gangplank and then, at last, they were on board.

Rounding a corner deep in the bowels of the ship, he stopped at a couple of doors. "Your quarters," he explained. "You've arrived early enough not to be split up. I guess that is important to you. Yes. Good." He ushered them into two adjacent cabins. "Grab a bunk and dump your stuff and I'll show you where you can get cleaned up."

The showers looked narrow but clean and very inviting. "When you're ready, come back to the purser's office and pick up your passes. Come and go as you please but don't be on the street after curfew. Got that?"

"Yes, sir... er... Mr Springer," said Hen.

The man laughed. "Keep you sirs for the captain. And Springer is not my real name. It's Kenny."

"Thank you, Kenny," said Roxanne. "We're looking forward to the trip."

"The thanks are all mine. I can never get enough entertainers. Don't go drinking, now, and miss the boat... literally." Kenny laughed at his own joke.

When he had gone, it was quiet except for the sound of what must have been the air-conditioning. Alice broke the silence. "Will we be sailing right by your home town, Tom?" she asked.

"Yeah, but I reckon we'll be too far out to see the coast, though."

"And we ain't going to see nothing much stuck down here," observed Nadia, examining the cabins. "It's good that none of us suffers from claustrophobia."

"Quite," agreed Hen.

Roxanne then got to thinking. "Those showers look great but we ain't got nothing to change into. I reckon a couple of us should nip into town and get some clothes."

"We have the rest of the cash from the Astoria," said Hen. "I don't know how much it'd buy, though, Rox."

"There'll be second hands shops. They're every other clothes shop in London – even in Oxford Street."

"Clothes for five?" wondered Hen.

"Nah, no problem. They're cheap. And you ain't seen *my* stash." Roxanne lifted her skirt and pulled out the note from the pocket of her knickers. As she did so, the cyanide capsule fell onto the floor. "Well that wasn't needed, was it? But *this* will be," She waved the note. "As you said, no point in taking British money to America, is there?"

Alice was not happy. "Look, guys, we're safe here on board – 'in America'. Going on shore is too risky."

Tom sighed. "I don't want to depress you, Alice. We might be on an American ship, but while it is in port it is not unassailable. If the British request permission to come aboard and arrest someone, the captain won't stop them. We're still under British jurisdiction until we are in international waters. And I wouldn't like to say how far that extends – it used to be three miles but I guess it could be much further than that with this regime."

"So it makes no odds if we are here or on land," declared Roxanne. "I propose that Hen and I go and buy clothes for everyone. Going as a group is what grabs the attention, right? I've got a tenner and I'm going to spend it."

"Agreed," sighed Hen. "We can't live without a change of clothes for the entire voyage. There were shops not far from the station. I propose we go right now and we'd be back long before curfew."

Alice wasn't happy but Nadia and Tom were much more relaxed with the proposal. She was outnumbered and so raised no objection.

When they had gone, Tom took Alice's hand. "They're very sensible and they will be extremely careful. Roxanne has managed to live safely in this world for months and the Nazis are not looking for us in Southampton – we're not important enough for them to put out a nationwide alert. Besides, we need a change of clothes; you won't want to be close to me when I begin to smell!"

"OK, you two, I'll make myself scarce while you have a snog," Nadia snickered and left before Alice could protest that a snog wasn't what she had in mind.

"Whatever else you could call it, that kiss on the stage wasn't a snog," muttered Alice. Tom smiled.

"She means well," he said. "She's right about one thing, though. There's been a thing between us all along, hasn't there? You were jealous when Roxanne started acting up to me."

"How'd you know that?"

"What you see is what you get with Alice Downey. And I like that."

"That's not fair. I can't keep *anything* secret."

"I'm glad. I feel the same about you... That's why that kiss just happened... But right now I think we have to play it cool. There's five of us and it's not going to work if two do stuff on the side. We don't want everyone making themselves scarce all the time. It's not that... It's not that I don't want you... But we can't – it wouldn't be right."

"No. It isn't. I'm sorry, I don't know what got into me – on that stage."

"It caught us by surprise – both of us. The music, the acting, it just served to break down the barriers we were putting up. But, in the cold light of day, I reckon we can control it."

"Of course," said Alice, curtly.

"Not forever, though. When all this – this adventure – is over, I'll come knocking."

"I'd like that."

Nadia reappeared, but not before clearing her throat as

she rounded the corner. "All done?"

"Look, Nadia," smiled Alice. "I like Tom but we're not going to do romance while we're here. It wouldn't be fair."

Nadia laughed. "Sad... but good plan. Too risky. You'll flip for sure and land in the sea!"

"We said we're sticking together, all five of us, and we mean it," said Alice, emphatically.

"Thanks, guys. I'd miss you if you – any of you – went..." Then Nadia broke into a grin, "Just let me be Godmother to your babies when the time comes!"

"Consider it done," laughed Tom. "But don't hold your breath."

33

Waiting for Hen and Roxanne was not easy. They decided to explore the ship and found a lot of it out of bounds to them but they discovered a few places where they could look out across the port buildings. Alice tried to spot Hen and Roxanne but people looked rather small and were all dressed in the same dull shapeless clothing and she couldn't make them out. She did spy the official at the gate who had rummaged through her bag. He was still checking people who were trickling into the dockside buildings. Those who were wearing their IDs pinned to their clothing he ushered straight through. She hoped that would happen to Hen and Roxanne when they returned.

The crews' quarters were definitely separate from those of the passengers but there was an inside lounge with soft chairs in which they could get coffee and cold food whenever they wanted it.

The time dragged by, slowly. Alice wished Hen and Roxanne would reappear soon; she got worked up. But Tom reassured her that there were hours to go before the curfew and not to worry. He found a pack of cards and taught them to play cribbage.

"All this arithmetic's mental," concluded Nadia. "Ain't you got anything easier to show us?"

But Tom urged her to persist. "All you have to do is count up to fifteen. I'll do the points."

Alice could do the sums all right but couldn't concentrate and made too many mistakes. She was increasingly on edge as the time went by.

Eventually, Alice muttered that she was going to go outside. She needed some air.

Tom knew what she wanted to do. "They won't be back just yet, Alice."

"I know. But I can't just sit and forget them. I don't know how you two can do it."

"No choice," reasoned Nadia. "If I worried about all the dumb things that happen back home, I wouldn't survive."

Alice fidgeted. "Guess not. But I haven't had your training." She didn't mean to sound callous.

Nadia understood and felt for her friend. "And I wouldn't wish it on you... Come on, then. Let's take a shufti."

There was no sign of Hen or Roxanne but what they did see was that the policeman on the gate had been replaced by a squad of intimidating black-uniformed men who were interrogating everyone at length. They had erected a table and were forcing people to empty all their belongings on to it for a meticulous search. Finally, men and women alike were subjected to a serious pat-down that made Alice shudder.

"That feeling people... That's positively indecent. I'm glad I'm not out there."

"Has Roxanne still got her cyanide on her?" asked Tom, concerned.

"No," said Alice. "She left it here... I think. What about Hen?"

"Nah. Nothing in his pockets."

They watched as a woman was led away from the squad to a waiting car. The man she was with was shouting but being held back. Alice found herself talking to God again. "These people are evil," she muttered.

"Best not watch, Alice." Tom took her hand, gently. "Come on, let's get another mug of that American coffee."

Alice allowed herself to be led away. She had come to this vantage point to settle herself, only to make it worse. "I wish they hadn't gone," she murmured. "I told them not to."

After what seemed like a lifetime, Hen and Roxanne eventually returned laden with bags of clothes. Alice overflowed with relief and greeted them as though they had been away months rather than a few hours.

"Got the undies new," announced Roxanne, throwing a bag to Tom and another to Nadia and Alice adding, under her breath, "Not quite what you're used to but they'll fit."

"That took half of Roxanne's stash," said Hen. "But then we found a charity shop and almost bought it up. There're two changes for each of us. I bag the blue jacket – unless you want it, Tom."

"This one?" asked Tom, holding up a double-breasted affair. "Too small for me and you know it is. I guess you bought some bigger stuff."

"We have," enthused Roxanne. "We hope you like it."

As Nadia rummaged through the bags, Alice went quiet before saying, "You were a long time." Roxanne registered Alice's anxiety.

"We were stopped. When we left it was the same police guy we met on the way in so that was OK; we were wearing our IDs and he let us pass out no problem. But when we got back he wasn't there; there were loads of others instead checking everyone going into the terminal. In fact, the police were everywhere. We think it's because tomorrow is the sailing day."

"What did they do to you?" asked Alice. "We saw them. They were searching everyone."

"Nothing," assured Hen.

"They were pulling loads of people out for questioning," explained Roxanne, "and sending some off to be strip-searched. I was just glad I had left the cyanide or they would have definitely found it if they had pulled me out."

"But they didn't search you?" asked Tom.

"No. Hen's good," nodded Roxanne. "He stood to attention and saluted. Right arm straight as a dye. I thought I'd better, too, although it made me feel kind of sick. They asked us why we were boarding the ship."

Hen laughed. "I told them I wanted to be in the élite forces and was required to get some experience of the world. A round trip on an American ship watching the 'other half' would qualify... The acting practice has been beneficial."

Roxanne explained that the Nazis wanted to see their tickets. Kenny's papers were endorsed, 'Out and return. No disembarkation permitted' and that satisfied them. "It was a scary moment, though," she confessed.

"Roxanne's a born actor, too," said Hen. "She was brilliant. When we get back to our world she'll have a stunning career in Hollywood – or else MI6."

To wash and change was bliss. Roxanne and Hen had even found some nightwear. Alice slept like a log; she was on a ship that belonged to friendly people and when they got to

America they would flip and telephone home. In the meantime, she would have Tom singing to her to come into his garden.

34

The following day – sailing day – the ship came alive early. The final consignments of cargo were being loaded and stewards were running in all directions. The five got up and dressed. They weren't sure what they should be doing but they found breakfast things set out in the staff area so helped themselves. Before six Kenny arrived, greeted them with a cheery smile, and told them they would be on stage that evening. The lounge used as the theatre with a stage and piano was out of bounds to the general public until the ship got underway and he asked them if they would like to go there and rehearse.

"Good idea," answered Hen. "I need to get acquainted with the piano. Come on guys, time for work."

Alice was happy. While a career on the stage was not for her, it was really good to be doing something. It was like having a real job – the first job she had ever had. And now that she and Tom had talked about things and she knew he was not going to fall for Roxanne, no matter how good she was at acting coy, she decided she would enjoy the performing.

At nine o'clock the ship's horn sounded – loud and deep. This was a signal for the passengers to board – the SS *United States* would set sail in two hours. The teenagers' spirits rose and the rehearsal became increasingly animated.

"We'll have to come up with a load more stuff if we are to do night after night on this ship," said Tom. "It'll be the same audience!"

"Yes. It seems that Mr Pottinger thought of that," said Hen. "He put a stack of sheet music into the bottom of my bag."

Alice felt a special sense of gratitude for the goodness in the human race. "There are some really kind and thoughtful people about. Even in this place run by Nazis."

"Yes," agreed Roxanne, "When things get hard for everyone, people seem to get less selfish and more generous. I've had so many people look after me here."

"More than on the flipside?" asked Alice.

"Definitely," Roxanne affirmed. "But I suppose it depends on who you get to meet."

"When we get back, I'll always be your friend," assured Alice. "I promise."

"Thanks, Alice. When we get back, I'll be glad of that. Back there, you have to be bold and actively find a role to play – it don't, just, come to you like it does here."

"But it's *here* you have to be bold!" marvelled Alice.

"Yeah. But it's a different kind of bold. In some ways, this type's easier – not so many greys."

Alice couldn't quite understand that. But she knew that Roxanne had never fitted in back in her birth world as well as she had here. It was an insight into how different people – she and Roxanne – could be living in the same country but not actually be what her dad would call "on the same page".

"I wondered why your bag was so heavy, Hen," remarked Tom, "seeing as you are smaller than me."

"I reckon you ought to wear your new blue velvet jacket, Hen, when you perform," said Alice. "You look really smart."

"I know, clothes hang well on me. My mother always told me so."

"*You're so vain!*" Roxanne sang. "You'd be wasted as a maths geek."

"Mathematicians can be performers as well," declared Hen. "Enough chatter. *Come into the Garden Maud.*" The ship's horn sounded a second blast as he played the introduction. Last call – the gangways would soon be removed.

Alice was just striking her 'hard-to-get' pose when the empty room resonated under the metal-heeled boots of three black-clad Sestapo officers. Tom stopped singing. Hen looked up to see why, and the notes ground to a halt.

"The Five Dimensions, I presume?" clipped the leading officer. "Your escape is over! On the floor! Face down! Hands behind your backs. Move!"

They were roughly handcuffed and dragged to their feet before being led out of the lounge past some amazed passengers and down the last-remaining gangway. None of them had said anything and Alice was in such a state of shock that it never occurred to her to call out. As they stepped off the gangway onto the quayside, the ship's horn bellowed a third time, and Alice saw the gangway was being raised and stevedores were removing the hawsers from the bollards.

35

Their handcuffs were repositioned with their hands in front of them and the five friends were marched through the terminal and forced into two black cars. They neither looked at one another nor spoke. Alice had never been so afraid. She thought of the suicide pill but that, along with all the rest of the stuff they had accumulated, was now on its way to New York.

They passed the railway station and Alice wondered if they were going to be driven back to London but the cars drew up at a brick-built functional-looking building with a large black lightning symbol over an arched doorway. The teenagers were half ushered, half dragged out onto the steps and frogmarched through the heavy black doors into a large marble-floored hallway bedecked with BUF flags and pictures of Mosley and Hitler.

In the centre was a stone staircase but they were led to the side of it and down a narrow flight of stairs to a lower floor with wooden-doored rooms to left and right. Hen was bundled into the first one and Nadia a second further on. Alice was taken off to the left. She did not see where Tom and Roxanne went – they were behind her. The room had a high window through which she could see clouds but nothing else. The door was firmly shut behind her and no sound of the outside world could be heard. In the centre of the room was a plain wooden table with two chairs positioned on opposite sides. She chose a spot against a white-painted side wall and slid down onto the plain wooden floor. All was quiet.

Alice sat cross-legged with her handcuffed hands in front of her, hardly able to think. At that moment she wished that fear stimulated 5D flipping but, of course, it had the completely opposite effect. Very soon, she was going to be interrogated and then suffer untold pain, and after that... Was there a life after death?

But the minutes extended into what seemed like an hour and she became conscious she needed to pee. She got up and walked about; the silence was deafening. *Why are they leaving me here? What am I supposed to have done? How much do they know?*

She sat again, her knees drawn up to ease the urgency of her bladder... and waited... and waited. Were they interrogating the others first? Or was the waiting part of the plan – get her rattled. She rehearsed in her mind what she was going to say: They had arrived on the day of the first performance from their parallel world. And then she would talk about that world as much, and as truthfully, as she liked. Alice knew she could not lie effectively – she could not begin to act

– so her only hope was that they believed the one lie that they had all arrived together on the same day and were taken in by people she did not know to a place she did not know. She hoped the others were going to keep to the same story. She could truthfully say that she had never been anywhere near the Astoria before. The thing that worried her the most was her association with the incident at The Voice. *I hope they haven't connected us with that place,* she thought. *Better not even think about it.* Alice was almost grateful that she desperately needed to relieve herself because it was becoming a major distraction.

After what Alice reckoned must have been hours, the door opened and a stout black-uniformed woman of indeterminate age strode in and stood at the chair beneath the window.

"Sit," she ordered Alice into the chair opposite. Alice did as she was told. The chair creaked under her weight. The woman took a sheaf of paper from a briefcase and a chunky pen out of a breast pocket. "Why are you here?" she demanded, without looking at Alice.

Alice shrugged. "I don't know." She didn't want to give anything away. The woman looked up.

"Don't take that attitude with me!" she barked, staring into Alice's eyes. Alice noticed her interrogator's eyes were green.

"Sorry," said Alice. "I really don't know why I'm here." Amazingly, now the interrogation had begun she felt better. "I need to go to the loo," she declared. "I've been here for hours."

"The lavatory? Well, you'll have to wait. Why did you come to Southampton?"

"To join the *SS United States* as part of our troupe of entertainers."

"Who brought you here?"

"I don't know his name. We came in a taxi."

"All the way from London?"

"Yes."

"Didn't you find that strange? A train would have been cheaper."

"There are five of us. We needed to get to the ship before it sailed."

"Who paid for the taxi?"

"I don't know. The ship, I guess."

The interrogation continued. At one point, Alice broke out into a cold sweat. She told them that they had performed in the Astoria on three occasions and, before that, they had been in their own world.

"Your *own* world! Explain!" demanded the woman.

Alice explained about 5D and exactly how it worked. That they had come to this world by pure accident and that, until they could find a way of flipping to get back, they had been forced to remain. All the woman now seemed to be interested in was the 5D; there was no mention of The Voice and no questions even about where they had been staying in Streatham.

After fifteen minutes, Alice again asked for the loo. The women said nothing and continued to write notes in her folder. Then she stood, opened the door, summoned a guard and instructed that Alice be taken to the toilet.

She was led back along the corridor. As she passed a room on her right she heard Nadia giving her interrogator a stream of abuse. She was using words that she had never used in front of Alice. The gist of what she was saying was that her world might be far from perfect but it was a darn sight better than this one if they treated people like she was being treated. Alice hoped that Nadia wasn't going too far, but the girl was not noted for her diplomacy. Roxanne had the biggest amount to lose but she was a good liar. Hen would be concentrating on the science. Tom? Tom could be in the worst trouble. She daren't let herself think of him. When they arrived at the appropriate door the guard took off her handcuffs, opened the door, ushered her in and slammed it to. There was no window – just a harsh light in the ceiling. The toilet, itself, was a simple hole in the ground and a jug and bowl and grubby towel stood on a low dilapidated table. Above the door, there was the inevitable spy camera which she tried to ignore.

Alice emerged to be taken back along the corridor and they met Tom being led, still handcuffed, in the opposite direction. Their eyes met and he gave her the faintest of smiles before he was dragged into a room to her left. At least it didn't appear he had been tortured at that point.

Alice sat alone in her interrogation room for what seemed like another hour. *OK God,* she said inside her head, *if you're there, do you care?* And then for some reason, all she could picture was Jesus being nailed to his cross and she shuddered. Believing in God, it seemed, didn't help when it came to being tortured. She put that out of her mind and began to hum some of the songs they had learned. She saw in her mind's eye the face of Tom pleading with her – as Maud – to come into his garden. And then... the kiss. Her first kiss. It had to count – neither of them had been acting. It occurred to her that if her life was to end in this place, at least she had known what it was like to have been kissed by a boy with a true heart. Her mother had always said that many people never got to be loved like she was – she was very lucky with her father. Alice knew that to be true – at school, many kids had complicated backgrounds. If that kiss was the only one she would ever receive in her short life, she would have experienced more than a whole raft of grown-ups. She would think of that kiss as she was dying and, who knows, if life didn't end at death, she and Tom might even be reunited on the other side!

36

Alice was thinking about her mum and dad and that they must be asking where she was by now when the door opened and a guard ordered her out and led her along more corridors and up a flight of backstairs. What were they going to do to her? She had shown no reluctance to answer their questions. *I've given them no reason to torture me. They've not asked me anything I didn't answer... have I?* The woman hadn't asked about anything except the Astoria and the fifth.

Then Alice found herself in a larger room with stools arranged around a central desk and a leather upholstered chair above which hung a picture of a stern-looking man whom she recognised as the current president of the British Republic. To the left of the desk stood a large BUF flag. Alice was placed on one of the stools.

To her great delight, one at a time the other four also arrived and were set on stools beside her. She looked down at her feet – they all did; this room was bound to be bristling with spy cameras.

"All stand," ordered a guard from the door.

Alice stood – she didn't turn round. An officer – clearly of senior rank – who looked remarkably like Donald Padget strode into the room and seated himself in the leather chair.

"Sit," barked the guard from behind. They sat. For a moment Alice thought this man was Padget. Had he mastered the 5D? He couldn't have – he didn't know enough about it, surely. That was why he needed the clinic and Prof W, wasn't it? Unless... Then the man spoke; he was not Donald Padget.

"It may be a surprise," he sneered with heavy sarcasm, "for you to know that we are already aware of your world."

You may not be Donald Padget, thought Alice, *but you are just like him – pompous, controlling and insane.* Alice took an instant dislike to him and then became aware of feeling more herself. It might have been something to do with the fact that they were all together again and seemed to have survived the first interrogation. This was dangerous, it would show on her face for sure. She looked at her feet and contemplated her shoes – she was still wearing the same pair of trainers that she had brought to London with her from Leeds.

The man continued.

"This is not the first time we have heard of the existence of alternative worlds – our scientists have long pointed out the possibility of a parallel reality. *Your* world, it appears, is only just catching up with the beauty and order of the true regime. I, myself, have always found the research rather fascinating." He appeared genuinely pleased. "I am sure our scientists would delight in having subjects like yourselves to experiment on," he gave a cynical laugh, and then changed his expression and almost roared with delight, "You will be taken to a specialist facility for further investigation."

He then called a junior officer and spoke to him quietly in what he thought was out of earshot of the teenagers – but he did not know that Roxanne was gifted with acute hearing. He was reminding his junior of the sensitivity of the situation. The *Five Dimensions* had been popular in London. They could not risk a protest – people were sensitive when it came to the treatment of young people. They were to be transported incognito; nothing was to be done that could spark any local revolt. Then he mentioned 'State Red' which Roxanne understood – it was a coded expression for an expected rebel attack. An attack, Roxanne knew, could spark an uprising on the lines of the one in Germany but, in this instance, one that could well be repeated across the whole of the continent.

"Stand!" ordered the guard. They stood. The senior officer swept out of the doors.

To Alice's astonishment, they were led out to an underground car park and then ushered, still handcuffed, into a white van with "Will's Whiter than White Laundry" stencilled on the side. The van doors were slammed shut. Groping about in the dark, they found some bundles of linen which proved soft enough to sit on as the van bounced its way through the Southampton streets.

They bunched up together as much as they could to prevent themselves from being thrown around. There was no way of knowing which way they were going – all they could see was a little chink of light through a vent. Alice hoped it would let in enough oxygen to keep five people alive.

Hen broke the silence. He kept his voice low so it could not be heard over the noise of the van. "You all OK?"

"Yeah," answered Tom. "The bloke yelled at me. He wasn't interested in where we were in London – just the fifth. I told him all about it as we agreed... right?"

"Right." This was Roxanne. "5D flipping's a big thing for them – that's all they're interested in."

"That man – the one in charge – he reminded me of Padget," put in Alice.

Nadia was angry. "He better not be up to the same trick! No one's getting my noggin."

"What happened there could have been much worse," observed Hen. "They must be pretty desperate to use a civilian van."

"They're scared," explained Roxanne. "The commander mentioned State Red. They know the situation is tense. It'll only be a matter of time before something triggers off an uprising.

The fascist oppression cannot last forever – no oppression can."

"That makes sense now," said Hen.

"So what do you reckon they're going to do with us?" asked Tom.

Hen shrugged. "Same as Prof W – experiment on us... Probably not kill us."

Nadia became a little calmer. "Not slice up brains, then."

"No... You know, I don't think, left to himself, Prof W would ever have done that," murmured Hen. "He was hoping someone would die of an accident but he wouldn't have risked breaking the law even if he had no moral conscience."

"And it wasn't ever going to get him anywhere, anyway, was it?" stated Nadia. "And these people won't get anywhere, either."

"Doing stuff to us just won't work, whatever it is," remonstrated Alice. "Threatening and doing bad stuff to me is the best cure for flipping I've come across. It puts me right off... *Where* do you think they're taking us?"

"Could be anywhere," answered Hen. "Some kind of facility where they can do the science but exactly where that is, we'll have to wait and see."

"You mean a place like the Winterford?" asked Roxanne.

Hen shrugged. "Maybe. Or some kind of lab... or

hospital."

"Unless we can escape first," mouthed Tom over the increased noise as they picked up speed. "I'm going to see if these doors will open."

"That is unlikely," said Hen. He was right. Tom's efforts on the bolts proved fruitless. They were firmly locked.

The journey took longer than any of them expected. They appeared to have left the stops and starts of the city streets and were on a long fast road. After what seemed like hours, the light from the vent began to fade.

"Ten o'clock," murmured Hen.

"I'm bursting," said Tom. "Aren't we going to stop for a loo break?"

"And I'm really thirsty," complained Nadia.

"I'm going to bang on the partition until they stop," declared Tom.

"Not a bad idea," concurred Alice. "What do you say, Hen?" They all waited for Hen's opinion.

After a few moments, he said, "Yeah. Let's all go for it."

Three minutes of constant banging brought the van to a stop. A man opened the back door and pointed a rifle at them. "Cut the noise, right! I'm not going to be slow to use this."

"I need the loo," yelled Alice.

"The what?"

"She needs a pee," translated Tom. "So do I."

They could see they were in a lay-by beside a major road. They were passed by other traffic but it was some distance off. It was getting dark and trees obscured their view of anything beyond. A second man came back. "Let 'em pee here. One at a time. It won't hurt. If they get up to anything then shoot them. I could do with one myself, in any case."

It was the first the friends had seen of their captors. Alice looked at Hen. Was this an opportunity? Hen gave a slight shake of the head – it was far too dangerous; he had no doubt the man would use his weapon.

The loo-break concluded, they were back on the linen bundles and speeding along again.

37

Hours later they left the main road and travelled along what felt like twisty country lanes with a number of right-angled bends. Eventually, they turned up a bumpy track and, after several lurches into dips, the van stopped.

The engine was still running as one of the men got out. Then the young people heard what sounded like garage doors opening in front of them. The van pulled forward slowly a few metres before the driver cut the engine and all was very still. The silence was broken by the call of an owl.

Finally, the back of the van was opened and the young people were ordered out. The men wore a dismissive expression; they looked bored or tired – perhaps both. A combination of fuel and farmyard smells hung in the air. Alice could make out the soft roosting sounds of chickens or some kind of poultry, followed by the lowing of a cow; wherever they were, it was rural. She took in what she now decided in the semi-darkness was a kind of barn. A farmyard didn't seem to go with the Sestapo at all; by all appearances, these men were certainly not the country type.

Hen picked up on the incongruity. "You like the country?"

he asked in his calm polite voice, but not without a hint of mockery.

Then a third man, looking more like a farmer, came in. "Reight, you tykes. Frame thissen. Reckon you're chuffed you got us outa bed? On yer feet," he ordered, in a flat-vowelled northern accent.

The hairs on Alice's arms stood on end – this was the first time she had heard a Yorkshire accent like this in a long time. This man was what her mum and dad would have called, "proper Yorkshire" – old fashioned and "salt-of-the-earth".

The van men asked him, "Where do you want us to put 'em?"

Alice shivered again and held her upper arms – the thought of actually being in Yorkshire was a bit of a shock.

"You look starved," said the farmer. "Here, get som'ut on yer," and threw her a blanket from the back of the barn. "Teenagers! No backbone these days... Now quit yer faffin and follow me. And don't think you can scarper because these men here – nice as they be – have got you covered."

He led them to a small door at the back of the barn. They crossed a courtyard, passed what looked like loose boxes to a detached shed around a corner The farmer drew out a key and fumbled with a padlock. He pulled the door open, then grabbed Roxanne roughly by the arm and swung her through the open door.

"Get in," he barked. Tom took a step sideways to avoid the door but the van men were on hand to stop him. Hen entered obediently – no sense getting beaten up – escapes had to be well-timed and now was clearly not the time. After Tom had followed them in last, the door was slammed behind him.

The five friends sat on the floor. It was dark and they couldn't see anything; not even the moon and starlight could get in – all the windows had been boarded up.

"Where do you reckon we are?" asked Tom.

"In Yorkshire somewhere, guessing from the man's accent. Sheffield?" suggested Hen.

"That man spoke like someone from further north than that – not Sheffield, but not Leeds either," ventured Alice. "Could be Wakefield."

"Wow!" exclaimed Nadia. "You're clever."

"No. It's just that I'm from Leeds. This means I'm near home but stuck in here, I might as well be a million miles away."

"If we could get out, though, we could make a bid to get to your house," suggested Tom. "The farmer thought you were hungry – he might be bringing us something to eat. If he came alone and we were ready for him, perhaps we could overpower him."

"Hungry?" queried Alice, "He didn't say anything about

food. Although something to eat wouldn't be unwelcome."

"What was all that about starving, then?"

"Oh, Tom. Starving doesn't mean 'hungry'. It means 'cold'. That's why he threw me the blanket."

Tom looked doubtful. Was he still in England? It didn't mean that where he came from.

"Even if we can get out of here," said Hen, calmly, "your home isn't going to be your home, is it? Not on this side. And, as we've already discovered to our cost, five people together are not going to find it easy to remain unnoticed. We're going to have to come up with a good plan."

"What if we split up?" ventured Tom.

"No way!" exclaimed Nadia. Alice sensed her panic and put out a hand to her.

"You're right," affirmed Hen, with confident reassurance, "there's no way we're going to leave you. We shouldn't even try to go it alone. We have to stick together... and, when we can, we will need to flip together... you do all *want* to go back to our side."

"Of course! As you said, my family isn't here," asserted Alice, strongly. "And anywhere is better than sticking around in this Nazi world!"

"Rox, what about you?" asked Hen. "If we got a chance, would you come back with us?"

"Well, they're on to me now. The Sestapo have got my name; I know too much to be captured. The uprising's going to happen... and *I* know when it's planned for. So it's probably best if I left – in the interests of the others."

"Shhh!" said Nadia alarmed. "This place could be bugged. Now you've told them stuff!"

"I doubt it," said Hen. "It's very unlikely. But I suggest you keep what you know to yourself in any case, Rox. Safer all round... Look, I don't think this is the right place to escape from. Not now. It'll soon be getting light and we're most likely in the middle of fields – it will have been chosen because of its isolation. Remember the rough track that led to it? This'll be only a stopping off point; there will be other opportunities."

"How much further are they going to take us?" wondered Tom. If this was Yorkshire, he was further north than he had ever been or ever contemplated being. Somerset had represented the north for him. "I never knew Britain was so big!"

"It isn't really. Not compared to, say, Australia or the USA," muttered Alice.

"Donald Padget is from America," said Tom, ruefully. "When we get back to our side, he may be waiting for us so he can take us there. It'll be out of the frying pan and into the fire."

"We've no idea what he's planning now," replied Hen. "We'll meet that one when we get back."

If he does want to take us to America, Alice thought to herself, *it'll only be the bits of us he's interested in,* but she refrained from voicing it. To reconnect with the prof had to be avoided. They would have to find safety with their families – or at least one of them – as soon as they hit the other side. "What we haven't tried," she said, "is flipping right now. If we did and arrived in Wakefield, I'd be nearly home!"

Tom took her hand. "Could you flip, Alice? I mean do you *feel* you could do it right now?"

She shook her head; they all knew the answer. Conditions had to be right and being imprisoned inside a cold and dark shed with empty stomachs was far from ideal. To flip, you have to feel free and in that shed, they certainly didn't.

38

It was barely light when the farmer returned. They had slept fitfully on the hard wooden floor – the shed was empty of all but the bit of bedding they had been given. The weather, if anything, had got colder and Alice had been glad of the blanket that smelled of dogs and exhaust fumes.

"Reight kids," said the Yorkshireman. "Bathroom. You've got half an hour. Girls first." Alice, Roxanne and Nadia were ushered from the shed under the watchful eyes of the men with guns. Alice looked about her. The land was flat.

"You from Doncaster?" she asked as casually as she could.

"Never you mind where I'm from..." replied the farmer defensively. "And it in't Doncaster."

"Nearer Wakefield then?"

"Yer too smart for yer own good, lass. Stop callin and get a move on."

So they were somewhere near Wakefield. To the south and west of Wakefield, it was hilly, to the north the city virtually joined up with Leeds, so it had to be to the east somewhere. Her mum and dad would have been just up the motorway – if they had not been on the wrong side of the fifth. In her mind, she traced the M62, the M1 and M61 into the centre of Leeds and then the road on to Headingley. How she longed to be there now. But she knew she mustn't attempt to flip without the others – they must all stay together. She tried to imagine how Tom felt being so far from West Bay, which seemed to be much nearer, at least in his mind, to France than Yorkshire.

Breakfast was eggs, toast and marmalade served by a woman in a kitchen in the main house. She spoke with the same accent as the farmer although she didn't address them directly – they definitely got the impression that she was not happy with them being there. She grumbled that there were more mouths than they had agreed to. Her husband, if that was who he was, told her to keep hers shut. The van men stood over the young people as they ate.

Alice had an idea. If she could just get the woman on her own away from the men, away from the guns...

"Excuse me" she addressed the woman in her best Yorkshire. "Have you got?... I need some..."

"What you on about? You talking to me?" the woman grunted.

"Yes. It's a... a female thing," she said, "Can I go to the bathroom again before we go?"

"Dare say," the woman shrugged. There was a certain

reluctance but she must have felt some gender sympathy – just as Alice had hoped. Inside her head Alice told herself, *Lying again. I'm taking advantage of this woman's trying to help me.* She felt bad, but...

The woman led Alice out of the kitchen to the bathroom.

The driver stood up and stopped them. "Where are you going?" he demanded.

"Never you mind. It's not any of your business," spat the woman.

"Go with them," ordered the other man who seemed to be the one calling the shots.

The woman turned and snarled at him. "You... what's wrong with you? Why have you brought 'em here?"

"Quiet, woman!" barked the farmer.

"Not our choice," said Hen in mock apology.

"Shut it!" said the boss man.

"Or what?" retorted Hen, aggressively.

Tom rose from his seat ready for a fight.

Hen beckoned to him to sit down. "Better cool it," he said. Now was not the right time. There would be a better chance later – at a service station with lots of people about, perhaps. Even if they managed to overpower these people, they wouldn't get far from the farm on foot. On the road or in a service station they could hide somewhere, or disappear into the crowd.

Tom nodded.

"That's reight," said the farmer. "We don't want no trouble here."

"But, I still need..." lied Alice.

The boss brandished his assault rifle and bellowed at the farm woman, "You want to take her out the back? Take her. But nothing stupid, you hear." The woman led Alice to the bathroom followed by the gunman. She gave her what she needed in full view of him and Alice shut herself in the bathroom while the gunman stood guard. She had tried but there was no way she was going to be alone to talk with the woman privately.

39

After breakfast, they continued their journey in the van, stopping only twice and on both occasions, it was in a quiet lay-by where they were obliged to use the verges – there was no one else to be seen and no-where to run to. They travelled for hours; they must be going further north, concluded Alice. Although the five had been given bottles of water, they were becoming ravenously hungry.

Eventually, the van stopped for a third time and the men threw the teenagers a parcel of sandwiches and tins of Coke. By this time it was late afternoon – they must have been on the road for coming up to nine hours. An escape plan still did not seem possible. They never stopped anywhere public and at least one of the men stood over them with his assault rifle whenever they were in the open air.

As they continued their journey, Hen had an idea and he got his friends tearing one of the sheets they were sitting on into strips.

"It's now or never. Next time we stop, I'll pretend to be sick. I'll take the one that comes over to me and you take the other, Tom. Keep close to him. Then you girls jump on them, too, and tie them up with these strips."

"What about the gun?" asked Tom.

"If we're near enough to them and quick they won't get a chance to use it..." reasoned Hen, "It's our only chance. They're never going to let us out anywhere public."

When eventually the van stopped for a fourth time, it was dark. The five pleaded to be able to get out and stand up and stretch their legs for a bit. The men ushered them out, warning them that they "didn't want no funny business".

Alice emerged bruised and exhausted into what she instantly recognised as the highlands of Scotland – the smell of the pines and heather-clad peat hills gave it away. It had to be because of the time they had been on the road. It was truly dark but the night was clear and the stars shone brightly. The tree-lined lay-by was surrounded by a bank on all sides and there didn't appear to be a light of any description – except for the stars – anywhere. *This is a good place*, Alice thought, as Tom and Hen were led to the bank to relieve themselves.

The girls were still beside the van awaiting their turn when Hen bent down and got to his knees. Tom turned to him but the man with the gun shouted at him to stand away. Tom stood as close to the man as he dared. Hen put his head almost to the floor and moaned. The second man approached him and ordered him to his feet.

Tom protested, "He's ill. Can't you see that?"

The man beside Tom lowered his gun slightly to study Hen and Tom took his chance. He lunged at him, hitting him fully in the middle of his back. Caught by surprise, the man staggered forwards losing his grip of the gun, which, to Tom's enormous delight, fell into the ditch. Almost at the same instant, Hen was up and storming the second man who was taken off his guard, too. He staggered backwards under the impact of Hen's assault and banged his head on the side of the van. Alice, Nadia and Roxanne sprang into action. Nadia leapt on Hen's victim, pulling him to the ground and, together with Roxanne, had him front down with his face in the gravelly tarmac, Nadia forcing him into an oily puddle. Roxanne pinned his arms behind him.

Alice was onto Tom's man almost as quickly. Hen took over from Roxanne and yelled at her to get the strips of the linen sheet they had prepared. She gabbled a bundle and threw them to Hen, then she helped Tom and Alice control their gunman's legs and they tied them together at the ankles and knees. Hen was having more trouble but Nadia struck the man in his side and as he doubled up Roxanne turned her attention back to him, grabbed a leg and tied one end of a strip to his ankle then looped it around the second ankle and pulled them together. Nadia knelt on the man's neck, forcing his face further into the tarmac. After that, he made no effort to prevent

Hen tying his hands. Tom and Alice had their man bound neatly, too. Alice told herself that she should not be surprised at the dexterity of Tom's knotting – it must have been second nature to a man of the sea.

They'd done it and no one was hurt!

They decided to put their former captors, trussed up, in the back of the van but it was not an easy thing to achieve as the men continued to struggle. Before they could get them in, however, they noticed lights approaching along the road. Although the vehicle was still some way off, it was time for the friends to leave – they would not have finished with the men before it arrived.

"Better make ourselves scarce," ordered Hen. Leaving the men as they were, they leapt a ditch, climbed the bank and plunged into the dark, dense undergrowth beneath the first trees.

The air was sweet with the scent of pine, and the realisation that they were free made it even sweeter – it was definitely the freshest air they had tasted in a long time.

"Which way?" asked Alice as loudly as she dared.

"Upwards. Through those trees," breathed Hen, coming up behind her. It was dark – almost too dark to see where they were going. Progress was slow. Hen called a halt so they could listen. They could hear the men shouting – presumably at each other. The second vehicle had stopped and it was turned so that its lights shone into the woods but the fugitives were up the slope and too far to the left to be caught in the glare. They heard the men continue to argue in words that would not be acceptable in Alice's schoolyard, let alone the classrooms, but as the five pushed up deeper into the trees, the voices receded. After a further fifteen minutes, they picked up the sound of the van's engine starting and watched its lights through the trees as it headed away up the road away from them.

40

The five friends fled up the hillside to where the trees were replaced with heather which made the climbing difficult but they ploughed on. It was dark but the sky was cloudless and a sliver of the moon shone bright enough for them to see the gullies cut through the peat with standing pools of black water, which reflected the stars.

At first, the going was slow but as they reached the upper slopes the terrain became easier and the hazards fewer. The wind caught them as they topped the ridge. Lights of houses in the next valley appeared below them.

Nadia stood on the summit and opened her arms and sang into the wind. "The hills are alive with the sound of music..." It was the escape of the von Trapp family again. They were free!

Alice breathed in the fresh, clean mountain air and, for the first time in days, she stopped feeling afraid. And then she flipped, hard and fast. Swept up into the grey world, she was soon pelting along the plane chasing the black spheres. Then, there they were – all four of her friends. She reached out her hand and Tom took it. Soon they were in line abreast and keeping up with the spheres. Free! They floated along for what seemed an age before Tom tugged at Alice's hand conveying the message that Hen was going to try to climb up the flat angled plane. Hen took the lead. It wasn't easy, but gradually they forced their way across the smooth grey surface by side-stepping; it felt more like swimming than walking.

Eventually, Hen looked up towards the horizon – an end to the grey expanse and the beginning of an even, pale blue. Alice gasped. *This is it! We're going home!* Once on the other side, they would be able to hitch a ride back to Yorkshire – back to Headingley and her family. But as they fought closer, the going became harder and soon they were making no progress at all. Tom was the first to lose all grip on the sloping surface and as he slipped down it he dragged the others with him.

Back beside the ellipses, they gained some kind of control again and there to their right was the vortex, bright and colourful. Alice was aware of the splash of colour as – released now from Tom's grasp – she fought to keep steady and controlled.

Her heart sank as she re-entered the 4D world. She was absolutely gutted. Why hadn't they made it?

The friends found themselves sitting on the bare hillside a few metres apart. Hen was the first to speak; he was not going to be overtaken by a sense of failure.

"Not bad, guys. Fast entry – controlled exit. We managed to stay together. Any scrapes or bruises?"

"None here," said Tom, knocking bits of heather from his clothing.

"But we haven't done it, though, have we?" moaned Alice, with a mixture of anger, disappointment and heavy sadness. "I thought we might get to it – the apex – but then it seemed to fight back." She felt tears wetting her cheeks in the cool wind.

"Yes," said Hen. "Perhaps we were not going about getting there the right way this time."

"I feel OK, though," put in Roxanne. "It could be worse. We're still free!"

"Yeah, man. We're free!" shouted Nadia. "And the good news is that Prof W ain't in this world. And here on this hillside there ain't nobody watching us – no monitors or TV stuff. We've got away; that's the main thing!"

Nadia had hardly finished speaking when they heard the unmistakable sound of a pack of dogs. This time they would not be able to hide. Their scent trail would be unmistakable and the baying hounds would soon be upon them; the beams of powerful torches were already darting among the topmost trees.

Hen looked down at the nearest lights in the valley below them. A farmhouse perhaps. But it was too far away – they didn't stand a chance if the dogs were onto them.

Nevertheless, they fled down the slope jumping down the gullies and tripping over clumps of heather. They just managed to skirt an area of bog that might have seen the end of them; it was dangerous. The joy of freedom was turning into a nightmare of hazards. Alice had seen horrible pictures of what hounds could do to a fox when they caught it. But the thought of disappearing slowly into a bottomless quagmire was equally horrifying. Would that happen to them?

As if it sensed her mood, at that moment, the moon went behind a cloud and the night became pitch black – impending doom was upon them. Alice collided into Tom who had suddenly stopped running, then felt her foot sink down into a squelching hole. Tom grabbed her around the waist and pulled her back from the mire; the miasma of rotting vegetation filled the air. Standing safe but still in Tom's arms, Alice realised that they had survived the bog – it was the hound option, then.

41

Nadia had found Hen and held onto him as he felt around for a way around the bog. "What are we going to do?" she yelled, against the strengthening wind.

"There's nothing we can do," answered Hen. "Just stand still... don't drown in the gloop. I am familiar with hunting dogs in Somerset and know how fast they can run... Except... I could try to lead them away from you. All of you, get in this stream bed and follow it downwards!"

"Oh. No," screamed Nadia. "We stick together, right? They're going to catch us all, ain't they? They won't settle for just one of us."

But before Hen could argue, Alice felt a heavy drop hit her face and then another. It was starting to rain. Ten seconds later and the heavens were rent by a huge shaft of lightning, followed almost immediately by the roar of thunder. They saw the lightning strike between them and their pursuers, and the dogs' barking changed from excitement to panic. Then a powerful wind sprang up driving the rain into their faces. Lightning struck again and through the din of the storm, they could no longer hear the dogs.

"Run," shouted Hen. "Down the stream bed." He didn't have to ask twice. They slid into a sandy-bottomed gully. The wind became gale force; everything was eaten up by the storm. The whole hillside had become like the gates of hell. *It's like something out of the Book of Revelation!* Alice told herself. Another bolt of lightning struck somewhere across the valley, sheets of stinging rain soaked them to the skin and, despite the running, they became incredibly cold but they kept going. Soon, the small stream turned into a torrent cascading over rocks and gurgling through tunnels.

Tom yelled to the others. "Let's keep to the stream. Go careful, mind." He continued to hold onto Alice; in all of this, he had never let her go.

"Agreed," yelled Hen, bringing up the rear. The stream had advantages. They wouldn't run into a bog unawares and they could feel their way even if it was dark, and down in the dip, they would be less visible from above. "This rain is brilliant, the dogs will no longer have a scent-trail to follow," shouted Hen. If they could survive the storm they might yet escape. They had hope.

They bunched up close together, helping each other over the stones, Tom exploring the way. He led them out of the stream bed as they encountered a waterfall. They climbed down the rocks beside it, rounded a pool, then followed beside the racing water as the stream grew wider and deeper.

After ten more violent minutes, the rain abated. The thunderclaps became more distant and no longer reverberated in the narrow valley but the lightning flashed bright enough for them to make out a bridge. They looked back up the slope and saw the lights of their pursuers on the ridge but they were much higher up and going up further, away from them. Against all odds, they now had a real chance to escape.

"That was scary!" uttered Nadia. "I don't do thunderstorms."

"It worked, though," laughed Roxanne, "didn't it?"

"About the only thing that could have done," said Hen.

"I'm soaked," grumbled Alice. "If we don't get to dry off, we'll die of something else."

"She's right," agreed Tom. "Exposure's dangerous. At least the wind has lessened."

Grateful, they found a well-trodden track that headed towards a drystone wall and a style. Beyond lay a field studded with clumps of wildflowers. In the dark it was hard to tell what kind they were – probably the thistles for which Scotland was famous. The footpath led to a copse further down the slope. Alice put her foot into something soft and warm; not a bog this time – just a fresh cow-pat.

"Yuk," she uttered. "Cow shit!"

"Or bull shit," quaked Nadia. She hated cows. She rarely got into the countryside – even though in Bristol she really wasn't that far from it. But on one of the rare occasions when she had gone on a country walk with the school they had been pursued by a herd of curious young cattle. It had been sufficient to put her right off them.

"There won't be a problem," reasoned Tom. "They'll be OK here. Just keep to the path; it's well-trodden and, whatever sort they are, they'll be used to people."

But they didn't meet any animals before they passed through a kissing gate into the copse. Nadia breathed a sigh of relief – she was so glad she was out of the field. On the far side of the trees, the moon reappeared showing them a dappled path through an undergrowth of nettles and long grass.

Finally, they emerged through another kissing gate onto a rough track that led to farm buildings and beyond that a farmhouse with a light in the porch; they had made it to some vestige of civilisation.

"What now?" asked Alice.

"Not much choice really," said Hen. "We'll have to throw ourselves on this farmer's mercy and hope he's not a Nazi sympathiser."

"And I'm starving," put in Roxanne. "Starving hungry as

well as cold."

Alice said nothing – she just approached a big oak door with an iron knocker and knocked. They heard a footstep and then the door creaked open.

42

A startled man in a check shirt and work trousers opened the door.

"Goodness!" he grunted.

He was about fifty or so, stocky and weather-beaten and spoke with a Scottish accent. "Look Mary what we have here. Five teenagers resembling drowned rats, or are you rats looking like drowned teenagers?"

"Excuse us," said Hen in his best English upper-class accent. "We got caught in the rain."

"And a few other things, too, by the look 'o ye," said a friendly well-built woman of the same age. "Well, let them in, Jamie. Don't keep them standing out in the cold."

"We're in a spot of trouble," continued Hen.

"Is there someone lost up on the fells, then?" the man's voice took on a note of alarm.

"No," spoke up Alice. "We stuck together. We're all here."

"Best thing you could do... So we'll not be needing the mountain rescue, then?"

"No."

The teenagers stepped inside a warm kitchen full of the wonderful smells of a dinner in the making. Alice held back - conscious as she was of the cow dung on her shoes.

"Ye're not hurt?"

"No. Just dirty. The cows - couldn't see it in the dark. Sorry."

"And ye've mired the other one, it seems." The woman laughed. "Nay problem lassie. Take off those silly tennis-shoes, or whatever they're called these days... Ye need proper boots for the fells, you know... So none of you is hurt?" Alice shook her head. "There's nay panic, then. First things first. We'll get ye warm and dry..."

Alice stepped back on the verge to wipe her feet in the grass to get rid of the worst of the cow pat and bog dirt and they all took off their trainers and socks; only Hen bothered with the laces. Then they padded into the warmth of the farmhouse kitchen leaving wet footprints that soon disappeared under the drips from their clothes.

"No boots and no kit either, then?"

"Sorry. Nothing," said Alice.

"Sorry? It's not me ye need to be sorry too. Who sent you out on the fells with nothing but town things? And no pack, either. They should have their heads tested."

"Right," said the woman called Mary, "I'll go and get towels and dry clothes. Lasses off to the bathroom. Follow me. Lads, get your things off here."

"Better do as she says," said Jamie as the girls left the kitchen. They had got down to their underwear when Mary knocked and passed towels and some of Jamie's stuff to her husband.

"This'll do for now," she sang.

It didn't take long before they were all together in the kitchen basking in the heat of a cooking range. The boys looked like young farmers with thick loose trousers and checked shirts, the girls wore things that made them appear dressed up for a fancy-dress party. Nadia looked like a doll somewhere in the middle of a superfluity of cloth made up of a flowered blouse and a plaid skirt twice her size and held in place by blanket pins at the waist.

"Stop starin', will ya!" she uttered, as Tom and Hen took in the sight.

"Just thinking you look warm and dry," said Tom, politely.

"Exactly," agreed Mary.

"Thanks," murmured Alice from underneath a lacy blouse and winter-weight brown pinafore dress that had a waist, although it never came anywhere near hers. "It is kind of nice."

They were plied with hot tea and then Mary's home-made broth with wedges of bread, still warm from the oven. They ate hungrily.

"Where have ye been staying?" asked Jamie.

"Nowhere. Just arrived," answered Hen.

"I can't imagine what your teachers were doing sending you out not properly dressed and without a light at night. And it was not as if the thunder wasn't forecast."

"We weren't *sent* out by anyone," said Alice because the next question would be who was in charge of them.

"We escaped," supplied Nadia.

"This is sounding like one of your crime novels, Mary," laughed Jamie.

"No. It's serious," blurted Nadia. "They were planning on killing me. Everyone wants my brain. I thought I was a goner for sure. But now I'm free! But in... in our world..." Nadia tailed off as a wave of emotion spread through her and she was away into the fifth. Alice caught her as she slipped from her chair in the direction of the Aga. The couple stood up, shocked.

"She's OK," said Hen. He tried to explain to the amazed couple. "She'll be back in a minute. It's just that she hasn't been free for some time. It's the excitement."

Nadia sat up. "Sorry," she apologised. "I just can't get

used to being free."

"Look, just what's going on?" demanded Jamie, alarmed.

Hen went into an explanation but he knew he had left them behind from early on. Mary rose from her seat and left the kitchen.

"We all get this fifth dimension," summed up Alice as Jamie reached for a pipe.

"Well you're safe and dry, that's the main thing," he said, slowly.

Mary returned. "They're on their way," she whispered into her husband's ear. "They said to give them half an hour or so."

"Who?" asked Roxanne.

Mary looked away. "You're safe. No need to worry."

"You called someone?" asked Tom. Mary shrugged her shoulders.

"How could you?" complained Alice. "You don't believe us, do you?"

"We know you're here to be 'looked after'." Mary said the words "looked after" in a deliberate tone.

Then the realisation took hold of Nadia. "You think we're off our trolleys?" she protested. "We ain't... Come on guys, I ain't hanging around waiting for them to take me back and chop me brains out."

"Sorry," said Hen getting up. "We have no choice. We can't be taken back into custody. Thank you for the clothes and the lovely bread and soup. You are very kind. But you will understand if we..."

"Clear out," finished Nadia, decisively.

"... take our leave," rephrased Hen, politely.

Alice was already out the door and finding her trainers, quickly followed by Nadia and Roxanne. Tom and Hen followed. "We'll send the clothes back when we get a chance," he said and then he, too, was gone. Jamie pulled himself up with the intention of trying to stop them.

"Don't touch them," ordered his wife, "you're not allowed to manhandle teenagers these days."

"Bah," said Jamie. "It's for their own good. Never made no difference when I was a bairn."

"Times change," said Mary. "And besides, it's not our problem. We've done our bit. They won't get far in any case."

The five ran up the road towards the top of the pass and when they had crossed a cattle grid they branched out left in the direction of a steep rise that Hen guessed, once surmounted, would put them in the next valley. Mercifully, the rain had ceased. Hen resolved to insist on doing the talking next time – at least not let Nadia explain it so bluntly. He thought they should just say they were lost and ask for directions.

They were still on the same side of the hill when they saw the lights of vehicles coming up the valley and turning into the farmyard. Topping the rise they took in what lay in front of them. To their dismay, there were no houses of any description visible – just fold after fold of hills set against crisp bright stars.

43

Prof W opened a text message. "Damn! That meddling American bishop has turned up and has sent for the ruddy police. What right has she to—"

"Every right if she can't find the sods," growled Padget. They were driving to the Inverlochie Estate following their arrival at Glasgow, Prestwick to which they had flown from London. "Your Mrs Brean know where you are?"

"No."

"But she knows of Inverlochie?"

"You make no secret of the place, but I have rarely spoken of it... And she has no idea where I am now... or that I am with you... You kidnapped me, remember?" He stared at the back of Wood's head as he sat next to a local estate driver from Inverlochie.

"But she may mention me under interrogation and then it'll only be a matter of time before the police check it out so we've got to find the kids and get them out of the country before the police arrive at my door. The sooner the better."

"Interrogation? About you? Why should the police

interrogate her about you?"

"Because they'll ask her about everyone and anyone who has been near your damned clinic. Unfortunately, these days, missing kids are rather important - especially if they've got families who love them. A pity, but there it is."

"I could go back to London and stall them," blustered the professor.

"Oh, no you won't. I don't trust you, Williams; not one little bit. And what makes you think your lying will help? These people are experts at detecting lies - and besides, you're useless at acting; you're like a frog trying to be a kangaroo - you might hop but that's as far as it goes... And you're a *frog*, Williams, nothing so grand as a kangaroo," snickered Padget, derisively. "In any case, you're coming with me to do the one and only thing you *are* good at; we still need you to do the dissecting - unless you don't think it'll work."

"Oh, it'll work!" exclaimed the professor, seething inside from being put down and insulted. But he kept his cool and continued, "However, with the police and everything..."

"Where you will be, you will have no need to fear the British police. I've got people on finding the brats, so, for your sake, just pray they will find them before the police do."

44

Alice shivered. Fortunately, the sun rises early during the summer in the Scottish Highlands and the night soon gave way to day but a morning chill lingered long in the damp air. At least they were still free, so far...

"We've got to get back to our world," Alice sighed. "We've nowhere to go - even if we find another house somewhere, we've no friends here."

"Agreed," said Hen. "In a matter of hours, these hills could be crawling with BUF police. Our only hope is to escape this world completely - at least for now."

Nadia looked at Roxanne. "What about the resistance, have they any contacts in Scotland? Could they help us?"

"Maybe but I wouldn't know where. And it wouldn't be safe for them to hide anyone, anyway."

"So when *is* this rebellion going to happen?" Nadia wanted to know. "How long have we to wait?"

"It's coming. We will be given the sign. We all know what we should do so that there is a countrywide uprising - all at the same time."

Alice protested. "We can't wait for that. We need to flip."

"But how're we going to feel like it?" Tom mumbled. "It's OK when you've just got free but the thought of a pack of Nazis assembling with their dogs just down there spoils everything. And when we were free last night we still couldn't get up to the top – the divide."

"You couldn't," Roxanne, reminded him. "It was you who dragged us all back."

"So we don't touch each other!" retorted Tom. "We'll each do our best. And good luck to those who make it. I doubt I will even flip in any case."

Nadia didn't like this conversation. Their fellowship meant everything to her at that moment. "Look, I know you all have a different take on this world but we ain't—"

"Right. We're *not* splitting up, Nadia," stated Hen, decisively. "No one is going anywhere unless we all go together. And we *have* to do it now... And we *can* do it," he added, quietly. "It's about getting the mind just right."

"And that means all five of our minds!" exclaimed Nadia. "I say, one for all, all for one. We stick together."

"We won't leave you, Nadia," promised Roxanne. "The five musketeers we will be."

"I was just saying..." said Nadia.

"You said right," confirmed Hen. "We stick together. We

have to get our minds in sync."

"And our bodies," added Alice. "If we climb the grey slope, like, marching – same foot, in time... And if we get really close together, arms around each other rather than just holding hands–"

"Then we are less likely to slip and drag the rest back down," said Nadia looking at Tom.

"Yeah. OK. Sorry guys." Tom sighed.

"No falling out," affirmed Hen. "Sticking together means sticking up for one another."

"Yeah," agreed Alice. "Once we start blaming each other we're doomed for sure."

"I bet Padget's blaming Prof W for losing us," muttered Nadia.

"I bet he is," laughed Hen. "How careless of him... Though, I guess, Donald Padget's not above assassination."

"Whatever we do, if... *when* we get back, we must make sure we stay free," pronounced Tom, solemnly.

"Absolutely!" Nadia thumped the raised turf above a gully. "If we managed to flip right here, would we be in exactly the same spot in our world? I mean here, on these hills away from anyone, it's not going to be much different, is it? Not like London."

"Agreed," said Hen.

"So, how're we going to get in the mood?" asked Alice.

"What would get you in the mood?" Hen asked. Alice thought for no more than a few seconds.

"A four hundred metre race!" she declared.

"Winning it?"

"I doubt I'd finish it. I didn't the first time I flipped; I was still on the back straight."

"For me, singing," contributed Roxanne.

"Sailing," put in Tom.

"You're right guys," said Hen. "But what can we *all* do that would get us going? Sorry Tom, no boat... or water..."

"Wanting to be home with the people that love us," volunteered Alice.

"Speak for yourself," sighed Roxanne, "my best friends are in this world."

"But we're your friends, too, ain't we?" said Nadia.

"That's *it*, guys!" exclaimed Roxanne. "All for one, and one for all. Would it work if we hold on to each other – arms around each of our waists – like we're never going to let go, and march in step faster and faster across this grass. If you're holding on to me – like you mean it, *really* mean it..."

"We *do* mean it," said Alice, almost in tears.

"All for one and one for all!" Tom punched the air.

"OK, guys," said Hen. "Grab hold, as tight as you can. Nadia and Rox, you go in the middle with Alice... That's it. On the count of three, we yell our motto and march across the grass getting faster and faster – follow Nadia's lead. OK?"

They all bounced about enthusiastically and then engulfed each other and formed the closest line they could manage – Roxanne feeling more loved and wanted than she had ever done.

"One, two, three, four!" Nadia chanted. "All for one and one for all!"

Behind and below them, however, their cries hadn't gone unnoticed. Half a dozen Statpo men, clad in their unmistakable black uniforms, were hurrying up the slope. The going was steep but they were fit and fast across the heather.

Unaware of their immediate danger, the cry of the teenagers intent on flipping went up loud and urgent: "All for one and one for all!" They kept chanting. They marched and felt Nadia increase the pace. Alice began to go first and the others sensed her vibrations and they, too, flipped. It was like a plane taking off. They emerged onto the grey slope together at pace and Tom, on the left flank, led them up the slope. They approached the horizon but, as before, Tom began to struggle. Yet the strength of the legs and bodies of the others forced him upwards and he got a second rush of adrenalin until, at last, despite his left leg being the weaker, he reached the top. But this time, instead of being a sharp right-angled ridge, it was rounded and smooth. Was this the right way back into their world?

Tom, still clutching hold of Alice, began sliding down the other side. They tumbled after him – Nadia holding Hen so tightly that she dragged him over the smooth summit, his feet no longer in contact with either slope. Held by a girl closer than he had ever been held, Hen regained his footing and joined the steady slide towards the left-hand vortex. Tom kept control and guided them past the ellipses and through the exit. They continued to cling to each other as they landed feet down on the grass, still marching. The place looked identical to the one they had left.

Where were they? Had they crossed over? Surely they had. Alice was about to shout in triumph when she felt Tom's arm tighten around her waist and, in the same instant, heard Nadia swear and Roxanne utter a cry of pain.

The story continues in book three of the Flip Trilogy:

1. *Flip! On the Edge*
2. *Beyond the Horizon*
3. *The Daisychain.*

If you have enjoyed this book, please recommend it to your friends
and rate it on Goodreads:
https://www.goodreads.com

and on Amazon:
https://www.amazon.co.uk/s?k=trevor+stubbs

If you can write a short review, too, that would be brilliant.

Trevor Stubbs
www.trevorstubbs.co.uk

FROM THE AUTHOR

Between 2008 and 2011, I spent more than two years working in Bishop Gwynne College in Juba in what is now South Sudan.

Next door to the college is a facility for girl street children – Confident Children out of Conflict[*]. The project grew from small beginnings when groups of girls living rough in the market attached themselves to a few caring people.

Children on the streets – especially girls – are very vulnerable, particularly in the hours of darkness. Although the temperature at night in Juba is relatively benign, virtually nothing else is.

The CCC compound has room for fifty girls but it is well over-subscribed. The aim is to see that the children receive trauma-care, security and the love they so desperately need, as well as proper food, clothing, medical care and school fees.

CCC relies entirely on charitable giving with grants from UNICEF and other trusts and gifts from individuals.

I give all profits from the sale of my books to CCC and I am delighted to report that these, plus other donations that I have received over the years, have resulted in my being able to send them a few thousands of British pounds.

My hope is that with the publication of this Flip trilogy, I will have even more to contribute.

Thank you for your contribution through the purchase of this book.

Trevor Stubbs. July 2019

[*]www.confidentchildren.org

The White Gates Adventures

by Trevor Stubbs

The Kicking Tree

Ultimate Justice

Winds & Wonders

The Spark

Meet Jack Smith (18) from Planet Earth - angry and drifting - and Jalli Rarga (17) from Planet Raika in the Andromeda Galaxy, struggling to be different from other girls.

Step with them through strange white gates into wonderful new worlds.

Adventure - Sci-Fi - Fear - Fun - Humour - Love

Explore outwards into the vast universe and inwards to the human heart where everyone matters.

Book Cover Design by Aimee Coveney | Bookollective
Cover Images copyright of Shutterstock.

www.ingramcontent.com/pod-product-compliance
Lightning Source LLC
Chambersburg PA
CBHW021422110726
47901CB00008B/2261